Gothic Appalachian Literature

Anthem Studies in Gothic Literature incorporates a broad range of titles that undertake rigorous, multi-disciplinary and original scholarship in the domain of Gothic Studies and respond, where possible, to existing classroom/module needs. The series aims to foster innovative international scholarship that interrogates established ideas in this rapidly growing field, to broaden critical and theoretical discussion among scholars and students, and to enhance the nature and availability of existing scholarly resources.

Series Editor

Carol Margaret Davison – *University of Windsor, Canada*

Editorial Board

Xavier Aldana Reyes – *Manchester Metropolitan University, UK*
Katarzyna Ancuta – *Chulalongkorn University, Thailand*
Frances A. Chiu – *The New School, USA*
Ken Gelder – *University of Melbourne, Australia*
Tabish Khair – *Aarhus University, Denmark*
Tanya Krzywinska – *Falmouth University, UK*
Vijay Mishra – *Murdoch University, Australia*
Marie Mulvey-Roberts – *University of the West of England, UK*
Andrew Hock Soon Ng – *Monash University, Malaysia*
Inés Ordiz – *University of Stirling, UK*
David Punter – *University of Bristol, UK*
Dale Townshend – *Manchester Metropolitan University, UK*
Jeffrey Andrew Weinstock – *Central Michigan University, USA*
Maisha Wester – *University of Indiana, USA*
Gina Wisker – *University of Brighton, UK*

Gothic Appalachian Literature

Sarah Robertson

ANTHEM PRESS

Anthem Press
An imprint of Wimbledon Publishing Company
www.anthempress.com

This edition first published in UK and USA 2024
by ANTHEM PRESS
75–76 Blackfriars Road, London SE1 8HA, UK
or PO Box 9779, London SW19 7ZG, UK
and
244 Madison Ave #116, New York, NY 10016, USA

© 2024 | Sarah Robertson

The author asserts the moral right to be identified as the author of this work.

All rights reserved. Without limiting the rights under copyright reserved above, no part of this publication may be reproduced, stored or introduced into a retrieval system, or transmitted, in any form or by any means (electronic, mechanical, photocopying, recording or otherwise), without the prior written permission of both the copyright owner and the above publisher of this book.

British Library Cataloguing-in-Publication Data
A catalogue record for this book is available from the British Library.

Library of Congress Cataloging-in-Publication Data: 2024937676
A catalog record for this book has been requested.

ISBN-13: 978-1-83998-678-9 (Pbk)
ISBN-10: 1-83998-678-6 (Pbk)

This title is also available as an e-book.

CONTENTS

Introduction	1
1. War and Diseases of Despair in Gothic Appalachian Literature	17
2. The Extractive Logic and the Climate Crisis in Gothic Appalachian Literature	35
3. Race and LGBTQ+ Rights in Gothic Appalachian Literature	53
Conclusion	71
Works Cited	75
Index	87

Introduction

"There is a strange awfulness about Appalachia that quickens the imagination," writes Guy Davenport in his 1968 review of Cormac McCarthy's *Outer Dark* (1968), drawing on the commonplace idea of Appalachia as a region distinctly other, distinctly gothic: a place replete with isolated communities, "hillbillies" and violent feuding families, a place to be feared.[1] The idea of Appalachia as monstrous other was fueled by travelogues and literature of the region in the eighteenth and nineteenth centuries, and further compounded by the American eugenics movement. Richard Knox Robinson notes, "For over 100 years the American eugenics movement used the hillbilly stereotype to justify its surveillance, categorization, institutionalization, and sterilization of what they called 'defectives'."[2] This othering of Appalachia and its people sat in direct contrast to the romanticization of Appalachia as a place where folk traditions and independence shaped local culture, turning the region into what Ronald Eller terms "a Janus-faced 'other'."[3] While competing ideas of the region still hold firm in the national imaginary, sentimentalism pales into the background as the notion of Appalachia as horrific other prevails, repeatedly reanimated in an array of cultural productions including John Boorman's notorious 1972 film adaptation of James Dickey's *Deliverance* (1970), Robert Schenkkan's play *The Kentucky Cycle* (1993), and J. D. Vance's controversial memoir, *Hillbilly Elegy* (2016).[4] This book is the first extended study of Appalachia's major gothic literature, exploring both its extensive reach and impact as it challenges and changes ideas of the region and its people.

Of course, like many places across the world, Appalachia is replete with legends and folklore, and all manner of gothic creatures populate the region's storytelling.[5] From the earliest Indigenous peoples to settler colonials, from slaves to their descendants, and the waves of immigration that continue to shape Appalachia, there are copious tales of shapeshifters, witches, creatures, cryptids, ghouls, ghosts, and monsters that haunt the region's storytelling.[6] The region's literature also turns to several superstitions, including the tree in Granny May's garden full of dangling "Multicolored glass bottles" to capture and contain the "evils" that might "come skulking over the far hills, out of the lightless hollers" in Taylor Brown's *Gods of Howl Mountain* (2018)[7] and the range of superstitions around childbirth such as the "cross/fastened to the pillow warding off haints" in Chanda Feldman's poem "But We Lived" (2018).[8] So, with all its superstitions, "haints" and creatures, there is little doubt that Appalachian literature offers a gothic playground. As Agnieszka Soltysik Monnet explains, "Inherently skeptical of the Enlightenment values that nevertheless underpin its critiques of traditional institutions, the Gothic interested itself in alternative epistemologies such as folk culture, family legends, and rumors."[9] Having first emerged in response to a period of significant social and political change during the Enlightenment, the gothic necessarily resurfaces in periods of socioeconomic and political turmoil, but as Monnet indicates, in cultures where "folk culture, family legends and rumors" flourish, the gothic is ever present.

Meanwhile, for Fred Botting, the "tensions between perception and misperception, understanding and misreading, fancy and realism, provide the condition and problem of gothic texts."[10] To that end, gothic tropes abound in a region so readily misinterpreted. Allen Batteau notes that "The image of Appalachia as a strange land and peculiar people was elaborated at the very same time that the relationships of external domination and control of the Southern Mountain Region's natural and human resources were being elaborated."[11] Othering a place and its people allows extractive industries to do their worst and the gothic provides Appalachian authors with a means to expose the extractive logic that has rendered parts of the region economic and environmental sacrifice zones.

Writing about the first industrial revolution, Naomi Klein saliently charts the emergence of expansive fossil fuel extraction and resulting sacrifice zones, places where "the black lungs of the coal miners or the poisoned waterways" are the prices "worth paying in exchange for coal's intoxicating promise of freedom from the physical world—a freedom that unleashed capitalism's full force to dominate both workers and other cultures."[12] Since then, vast areas of the Global South and parts of the Global North including areas of Appalachia, and more recently the Bakken formation in Montana and the Canadian Tar Sands, to name but a few, have been sacrificed, places Klein argues "privileged people" have easily ignored, seeing them as "hinterlands, wastelands, nowhere."[13] Specifically in relation to Appalachia, Bill McClanahan outlines the devastating impacts of extraction which includes the flattening of over "500 mountains" and the burial of "over 2000 miles of streams."[14] He argues that at its core, extraction is "an ecologically subtractive force, in that it does not merely *extract* value and material, leaving behind an acceptable facsimile of what was, but instead *subtracts* from all it encounters." In this form of subtraction, McClanahan argues, "what is left behind is often left empty; in emptiness is ecological and existential isolation, and in isolation, again, is horror."[15] Emerging from a significant sacrifice zone in the United

States, gothic Appalachian literature is deeply attuned to extractivism and its attendant horrors. So, while Appalachian folklore captures the imagination of its authors, they also turn to gothic tropes not because Appalachian culture is intrinsically monstrous and full of creatures who stalk the woods and lurk in shady crevices, but because the gothic illuminates hidden monsters and everyday horrors, historical and contemporaneous, including extraction and environmental degradation.

Gothic Appalachian literature is not merely a means to represent the horrors of an extractive logic. In her seminal work on the American gothic, Teresa Goddu recognizes that "the gothic, like all discourses, needs to be historicized." Only then, she argues, will "the horrors of history" be fully "articulated."[16] By necessity, historizing the Appalachian gothic lays bare its intrinsic connections to both the South and the nation through shared historical horrors. Goddu outlines how the American gothic rose "out of the nation's 'historical horror' including 'revolution, Indian massacre […] the transformation of the marketplace' and 'slavery'." From the earliest encounters between Indigenous people and explorers, encounters that brought the first Black people into the region in the 1500s, Appalachia has a long and diverse history, rife with the gothic horrors Goddu outlines.[17] Moreover, at the national level Goddu contends that the South and its "gothic doom and gloom" exists as "the nation's 'other'," in essence "the repository for everything from which the nation wants to disassociate itself," a "benighted South" cast as the host of the nation's "irrational impulses."[18] More recently, Eller further troubles the idea of the nation's gothic, wondering if "Appalachia may […] have replaced the benighted South as the nation's most maligned region."[19]

Eller's question opens a debate about where the Appalachian gothic sits in relation to nation and region, and a broader question about the definition of Appalachia, which is a highly debated and sometimes fractious issue. Richard Straw argues that "it is made up of a generally core area: West Virginia, southwestern Virginia, eastern Kentucky, eastern Tennessee, western North Carolina, and the northern mountains of Georgia."[20] In contrast, the Appalachian Regional Commission (ARC) offers a wider, official definition of Appalachia which it breaks down into five subregions, ranging from New York State at its northernmost point, down to northern Alabama and Mississippi, a diverse region, as Dwight B. Billings explains, that is "composed of portions of twelve states."[21] ARC notes that in 2021 Appalachia's population was 26.3 million, spread across rural and urban communities, the largest urban centers including Pittsburgh and Knoxville.[22] Additionally, writing in 1990, Batteau recognizes Appalachia as much a "literary and political invention […] than a geographical discovery."[23] I do not intend to enter this ongoing debate, nor do I wish to offer any radically new understanding of what constitutes Appalachia. I largely deal throughout the book with literature and poetry from the central and southern subregions of Appalachia, but I also make turns to the literature of the northern subregions, particularly in Chapter 3 when I discuss fracking.

Yet how does the debate about Appalachia inform the idea of an Appalachian gothic? Leigh Anne Duck suggests that "In its contemporary profusion, the gothic is impossible to locate" and "accounts of a national or regional gothic" can "never rest securely."[24] If Duck is correct, and since Appalachia means something different to various groups, there may be no set idea of an Appalachian gothic. However, recurring issues in Appalachian literature, including turns to the horrors of war and extraction, demand to be considered as forming an Appalachian gothic, with all the caveats of its intrinsic links to both the South and the nation. Indeed, much critical work has been undertaken to present Appalachia not as a place apart but as a region deeply connected to the nation, so while this book argues for the Appalachian gothic, it does so by engaging with the ways the region's gothic is shaped by a national gothic.[25] Reading the Appalachian gothic along these lines means understanding the region in ways that problematize ideas of Appalachia as a monolithic entity, defined exclusively by white, heteronormative, conservative culture, moving instead to engage with the region's diversity across time.

I last wrote about gothic Appalachian literature before the 2016 U.S. presidential election and since then a new pattern has emerged, what I term here a distinct post-Trump moment in Appalachian literature, a deeply gothic moment as Appalachian authors from diverse backgrounds create a dominant and recurring refrain against the 45th president. The ascendancy of Trump to the White House and the repeated support he received in parts of the region in the 2020 election has led to a renewed discussion of Appalachia as other, a place sardonically labeled "Trump country," or what Billings terms "Trumpalachia."[26] Billings explains how in the wake of Trump's election win, large parts of the media and significant parts of the Democratic Party presented Appalachia as "the single cause of a national political disaster."[27] Appalachia became a convenient scapegoat, viewed as single-handedly carrying Trump to the White House. As Alan Maimon outlines, after Trump's win "writers and commentators, almost exclusively from Blue State America, set their gaze on Appalachia to ask variations of the same question: *How could you have let this happen*? Forget that Pennsylvania, Michigan, and Wisconsin were the states that swung the election to Trump."[28] While Trump gained wide support across many Appalachian states, Billings and Maimon compellingly highlight the media's failure to recognize the more nuanced political picture across the region and the active opposition to Trump in Appalachia. Appalachia has long been misrepresented in the national imaginary and many of its authors have long challenged those reductive stereotypes, but Trump's 2016 win has galvanized Appalachian authors with several taking direct aim at Trump and his baiting of the far right with policies that stoke culture wars and threaten and overturn hard-won equal rights.[29]

In Joy Castro's *Flight Risk* (2021), set in West Virginia and Chicago, the overwhelming emotions that Isabel Morales feels about Trump's 2016 win capture the fear, horror, and anger that runs throughout the Appalachian post-Trump moment. She thinks it was "a nightmare of the absurd […] come true," just "as if the world were collapsing." Isabel "knew what monsters looked like, and now a monster was in charge."[30] A monster at the top of American power makes it harder for Isabel to face her other demons in a novel where the monstrous takes several forms. In her edited collection on what she labels "Trump-era horror," Victoria McCollum notes that "in the Trump-era" there has been an "acceleration" of the horror genre across film, television, and culture.[31] Appalachian literature has responded in turn to the atypical 45th president, with Trump and his politics casting a gothic shadow over several short stories, poems, and novels that deal with intersectional concerns including the climate crisis and LGBTQ+ rights. Given the alignment of Trump with Appalachia, Trump's legacy in terms of the U.S. Supreme Court and the possibility of further limitations on equal rights as he runs again for the 2024 presidential election, it is vital to engage with how Appalachian authors respond to the multiple threats posed by his far-right policies. I explore this post-Trump moment in Chapter 2 with a specific focus on Trump's election win in relation to the climate crisis, notably the Tennessee wildfires of 2016, and in Chapter 3 where I consider equal rights and the region's LGBTQ+ fiction.

The chapters predominantly focus on contemporary Appalachian writers to trace the most recent strains of the gothic, including the post-Trump moment, because while Appalachian authors have much to wrestle with in terms of history, they also deploy the gothic as they work through the multifarious challenges of the present and in some cases the impending future. As Monnet suggests, while the gothic was "Once considered escapist or closely linked to fantasy," it "has recently begun to be explored for its material concerns and engagement with real-world matters."[32] So, from the opioid and meth crises to the erosion of LGBTQ+ rights and the existential threat of the climate crisis, contemporary Appalachian literature seethes with real-world gothic horror and terror, illuminating the parts of the region that are consistently obscured by reductive stereotypes.

Although the chapters largely explore contemporary literature to examine the most recent and recurring strains in gothic Appalachian literature, it is also important to engage here with earlier Appalachian writers to outline a broader history of the region's gothic literature. In this introductory overview, as well as in the chapters, I do not provide an exhaustive account of all Appalachian gothic literature, a task beyond the limits of this book. Instead, the authors and texts I turn to are illustrative of the Appalachian gothic but should not be taken as a comprehensive list of all authors, texts, and topics that form the Appalachian gothic.[33]

The Appalachian Gothic: From Early Travel Writing to the Twenty-First Century

Appalachia was first viewed gothically through the lens of early travel writers, and Katherine Ledford provides a useful categorization of the three major periods of travel and exploration narratives across early Appalachian history, narratives "from European colonial exploration (1660–1720), the first systematic commodification of the mountains (1720–1800), and sustained settlement of the region (1800–50)."[34] In the first wave, "men persistently characterized the mountains as adversarial, unnatural, and out of control," a violent landscape that stood as an affront to colonial explorers.[35] Time and again in gothic literature, Botting argues, "Mountains are craggy, inaccessible and intimidating; forests shadowy, impenetrable […] Nature appears hostile, untamed and threatening: again, darkness, obscurity and barely contained malevolent energy reinforce atmospheres of disorientation and fear."[36] If "disorientation and fear" were the hallmarks of early Appalachian exploration and travel writing, then control and plunder marked the next wave.

Ledford notes that in this second period, as the "landscape turned into a valuable commodity […] settlers were a potential barrier between the explorers and exploitation of natural resources."[37] It is vital to remember that in this period inhabitants were not only settler colonials but also the Indigenous people of the region, composed of a range of tribes including the Cherokee and Choctaw who in the third wave were violently removed from the land in huge numbers to make way for more settlers, the very settlers who would themselves come to be othered, considered at best, if inaccurately, as out-of-touch with modernity in their maintenance of traditional folkways, and at worst as degenerate "hillbillies," rural, backward, and menacing.

In the years after these waves of travel writing, the region's authors would grapple with the competing constructions of Appalachia, including Rebecca Harding Davis whose Civil War short stories, alongside her most well-known story, "Life in the Iron Mills" (1861), push back against simplified, reductive misreadings of Appalachia. In her searing critique of industrial life in Wheeling, Virginia, in "Life in the Iron Mills,"[38] where there are "slimy pools on the muddy streets," an engulfing "foul vapor" and "smoke […] clotted and black" cloaks everything, Davis was a forerunner for subsequent Appalachian writers who have sought to convey the impacts of progress.[39] While the story was lauded for its realism, it is also a profusely gothic tale. As Davis spins her story of the ironworker, Wolfe, a thwarted artist, and the lives led in this oppressive, industrial town, the unnamed narrator makes explicit her desire to take readers "into the thickest of the fog and mud and foul effluvia."[40] In this nightmarish space, gothic tropes abound from grotesque Deborah with her "ghastly" face and deformed body that aches "from standing twelve hours at the spools," to the mills for rolling iron where fire appears in every "horrible form" and workers look "like revengeful ghosts."[41] Davis deploys these gothic tropes to write back against environmental and human degradation, exposing the horrors of progress that are all too often hidden from those who benefit the most from socioeconomic prosperity.[42]

Whereas Davis complicated ideas of Appalachia in her fiction, one of the region's earliest writers, John Fox Jr., is commonly associated with the "southern mountaineer motif" that he depicted across several works, including *The Trail of the Lonesome Pine* (1912), in which star-crossed love between mountain girl June Tolliver and northern geologist Jack Hale plays out against a backdrop of feuding families.[43] Best-selling Fox heavily contributed to caricatures of the region and its people, yet performances of *The Trail of the Lonesome Pine* are an annual event in Big Stone Gap, Virginia, and the popularity of Fox's version of mountain life is based on the ongoing consumption of Appalachia as a place apart.[44] Emily Satterwhite suggests that even at the time of publication, readers were drawn to the tale by a "hunger for the authentic" that "fed a desire to visit the primitive."[45] This desire to see Appalachia as primitive other means, for Satterwhite, readers often miss Fox's wider critique of the boom and bust cycles of an extractive logic.

Indeed, when Hale, who surveys the land for coal at the start of the novel, witnesses the subsequent coal boom, he does so with "grim satisfaction." The boom is like an "avalanche sweeping southward; Pennsylvania was creeping down the Alleghanies, emissaries of New York were pouring into the hills" and it creates a "rush of madmen. Horses and mules were drowned in the mud holes along the road, such was the traffic and such were the floods."[46] The boom creeps, monstrously enveloping the area, a crushing force that drowns all in its wake: a worrying portent for what this monster will do for profit. Fox certainly trades in Appalachian stereotypes, but he is also attuned to the destructive, vampiric patterns that underpinned the growth of the nation. As David McNally explains, "Capitalist market-society overflows with monsters" and those monsters appear in all manner of Appalachian texts that engage with the socioeconomic forces that turned parts of the region into sacrifice zones.[47]

Take for example the infrastructural brutalism in Louise McNeill's *Gauley Mountain: A History in Verse* (1939) where in "Oil Field" oil derricks appear "Like windmill ghosts arisen/To haunt Old Verner's land"[48] or in "Deserted Lumber Yard," where we find a "bone yard of [...] pines," a ghostly remnant of deforestation.[49] Of course, the impacts of an extractive logic devastate not only the environment but also the lives and well-being of residents and workers. As Dolly Hawkins contemplates in Myra Page's proletariat novel of the 1930s, *Daughter of the Hills* (1950), "who among us had not found the shadow of mine death across" the "doorstill."[50] Appalachian literature is littered with the deaths underpinning progress and those texts are too many to attempt to cover here in any justice, but it is worth mentioning Hubert Skidmore's *Hawks Nest* (1941), a novel based on the Hawks Nest disaster in the early 1930s near Gauley Bridge, West Virginia.

The Hawks Nest Disaster is one of "the largest industrial disasters in U.S. history" where "Hundreds of miners, most of them African Americans, died from silicosis, a disease caused by the embedding of silica dust in the lungs," as they dug a tunnel "to channel water to a hydropower plant, which in turn would power Union Carbide's electro-metallurgical plant in Alloy, West Virginia."[51] Skidmore's proletariat novel focuses on the workers who, in the middle of the Great Depression, arrived in their thousands to work on the project and their individual experiences, particularly the racism faced by Black workers. Writing more broadly about the migration of Black workers from the Deep South to Appalachia, Karida L. Brown highlights that between "1990 and 1940, the black population in central Appalachia nearly tripled, from approximately 40,000 to early 115,000 inhabitants."[52] Skidmore's novel does much to highlight both Black migration into Appalachia in this period and the continued inequalities that Black families found there. In his work on the Hawks Nest disaster, Tom Douglass notes that "Of the 1,488 men who worked inside the tunnel, 1,129 were African Americans, and they would represent more than three-quarters of the men who would die."[53] Skidmore underlines throughout the ways workers were regarded as collateral damage as the project pushed on despite obvious signs workers were being exposed to harmful toxins. He writes, "New men quickly replaced the ones who were fired when the emaciated bodies could no longer man the drills, and any mucker who staggered was sent home [...] and then, if he was not able to return to the hole, another took his place, for all crews were kept at capacity, all work went on unremittently."[54] Skidmore's rediscovered novel about the true cost of energy production tells a gothic tale of the unremitting nature of "modernity's monstrosities," part of what McNally terms "the capitalist grotesque" that feeds on an extractive logic.[55]

INTRODUCTION

As I have already indicated, the Appalachian gothic is not limited to extraction. Drawing from the broader American and southern gothic forms, the Appalachian gothic also appears in places where authors critically examine their, and/or their characters' relationship to place, questions that lie at the center of two of the most significant Appalachian novels of the twentieth century, Thomas Wolfe's *Look Homeward, Angel* (1929) and Harriette Arnow's *The Dollmaker* (1954). In both novels, Wolfe and Arnow explore modernity, Wolfe in the changing world of his hometown, Asheville, North Carolina, and Arnow in the experiences of her Kentuckian Nevels family as it adapts to life in Detroit.

In Wolfe's novel, as central protagonist Eugene Gant struggles to reconcile his attachments to place and people, especially his dead brother, Ben, whose ghostly presence haunts Eugene, the novel takes on decidedly gothic tones, and Darlene Unrue in particular has reflected on the array of "archetypal Gothic images" that appear throughout *Look Homeward, Angel*. It shares, she argues, "significant elements of both Southern and Gothic setting [...] a quest, imprisonment, a ghost, and themes of isolation and fear of annihilation."[56] Indeed, when Eugene's mother, Eliza, thinks of her young son, she remembers looking into his "dark eyes" just after he was born, knowing "that in her dark and sorrowful womb a stranger had come to life, fed by lost communications of eternity, his own ghost, haunter of his own house, lonely to himself and the world."[57] Eugene's haunted self, or his alienation, exists in a changing, modernizing Appalachia and Wolfe's concerns about modernity connect him not just to William Faulkner but to modernist writers more broadly in the interwar period.[58] Indeed, at once an Appalachian and a southern writer, Wolfe should also, as Jedidiah Evans suggests, be read in transnational contexts, but closer to home, and over two decades later, Arnow's *The Dollmaker* would also yearn, through central protagonist Gertie Nevels, for a bucolic, Appalachian past devoid of the region's complex history.[59]

In Arnow's much-lauded novel, *The Dollmaker* (1954), gothic horrors proliferate as the Nevels family adjusts to life in Detroit after leaving their Kentucky home behind. From the moment Gertie Nevels arrives in Detroit with her children, she is appalled by "the blurred buildings, the smokestacks, the monstrous pipes wandering high above her."[60] The industrial city is every bit the horror show she anticipated and much of the novel depends on a rural/urban divide as Gertie harbors the dream of a self-sustaining farming life she was forced to relinquish to support her husband's fantasy of limitless job opportunities in the urban North, a fantasy that saw waves of migration out of the South and Appalachia in the twentieth century. Max Fraser notes that between 1900 and 1975 "somewhere around eight million poor white southerners" undertook out-migration.[61] In the same period, the Great Migration saw significant numbers of Black people moving progressively out of the South and Appalachia. Indeed, the Mississippi-born Black author William Attaway depicts the journey of three young black men from Kentucky to Pittsburgh in *Blood on the Forge* (1941). For John Claborn, in Attway's novel "The Kentucky landscape is neither wholly a pastoral ideal nor an anti-pastoral reality; it is marked by both natural beauty and racial violence, doubling as safe haven and potential lynching site."[62] In contrast, Gertie's Kentucky memories elide segregation and racial violence, as well as the profound impacts of modernity and industrialization.

As Steve Mooney outlines, by the 1940s Kentucky had "seen the initial rise and fall of the machine age in the hills, and with it the capitalist wage-labor system that created a world of dependency that represents the very opposite of self-sufficiency."[63] Coal companies in particular expanded exponentially in Kentucky and other parts of Appalachia in the first part of the twentieth century, and Willian H. Turner notes that "The influx of Blacks [...] into the coal fields of central Appalachia reached its peak in the 1920s," all changes that Arnow's novel overlooks.[64] Gertie's memories of her Kentucky home too easily forgo the changes already underway and even if her piece of agrarian heaven still existed when she and the family left, the changes to agricultural practices in the early decades of the twentieth century would see small-scale, subsistence farming becoming increasingly difficult as big ag and industrial-scale farming became the dominant agricultural model, a shift felt as acutely in parts of Appalachia as in other farming communities across the nation.

Industrial-scale farming is at the heart of Wilma Dykeman's *Return the Innocent Earth* (1973). Inspired by her marriage to an heir of the Stokely canning company, the North Carolina author writes of the trials and tribulations of the Clayburn family, owners of a successful canning company in Churchill, North Carolina. Readers pick up the Clayburn family in their midwestern headquarters run by ambitious Stull, whose avarice sees him working with Lex Morrison of "national Commercial and Botanical Research Lab" to develop a new spray that will retard the growth of plants on the vine, all in a bid to get "the edge [...] in next year's market."[65] Narrator Jon Clayburn, Stull's cousin and whose parents founded the company, casts Stull as voracious monster, prepared to do anything for the bottom line. Jon dismally reflects on the family's changed approach to the land, recalling how at one time "the Clayburns treated the land as if it were a deep, warm, fertile woman worthy of all the care they could lavish," but now, he recognizes, their business model means "the using is all."[66]

Intermittent gothic moments enhance the sense of ruin, as when Jon, back in Churchill, visits the Rathbone home that "once sat in a tiny clearing surrounded by a canopy of forest," a place once rich in biodiversity but now "a graveyard of rotting tree laps and jagged stumps" ravaged by the local sawmill,[67] or when Jon and Lex discover that the new wonder spray has failed and "the beans that" were "supposed to be green" are, instead, "pale and grayish. They dissolve like pudding" and every case must be "bulldoze(d) [...] underground."[68] To that end, the gothic reveals the price of relentless growth and Dykeman was "an early and active opponent of strip mining," as well as deforestation and aggressive agricultural practices.[69] In *Return the Innocent Earth* and across her writing, Dykeman was also a vocal proponent for racial equality, with Oliver Jones considering "her early advocacy of equal rights for blacks as one of her major literary contributions."[70]

It was during the Civil Rights era that Nikki Giovanni rose to prominence in the Black Arts Movement and the Knoxville-born poet continues to produce searingly political poetry that talks to the wider experiences of Black Americans in the United States. In her wake, several Black Appalachian poets have emerged that similarly address the wider concerns of Black Americans while also working through their connections to a region that is mistakenly read as monolithically white. Indeed, poet Frank X Walker founded the "Affrilachia" movement to draw attention to Black Appalachians and their culture, including fellow poets and writers such as Nikky Finney, doris davenport, and Crystal Wilkinson. As Black Appalachian poets and authors depict the complex intersections of race, violence, class, gender and sexuality, whether they identify as Affrilachian or Appalachian, or neither, as in the case of bell hooks who acknowledged her Appalachia roots without laying claim to a regional label, they, like many Black American authors across the United States turn repeatedly to gothic tropes. For Maisha L. Wester, Black writers "revise" gothic tropes "in unique ways to both speak back to the tradition's originators and to make it a capable and useful vehicle for expressing the terrors and complexities of black experience in America."[71] Moreover, in the case of Appalachia's Black writers, they also deploy the gothic as they work through the complexities of living in a region whose stereotypes erase them.

Of course, the author perhaps most aligned with the Appalachian gothic is Cormac McCarthy. I began this introduction with Guy Davenport's assessment of Appalachia's "strange awfulness" in his review of McCarthy's *Outer Dark*. Certainly, the gothic is a dominant strain across McCarthy's early Appalachian novels, and while Lydia Cooper more firmly locates McCarthy's early fiction within the southern gothic, she notes that "One element of the gothic aesthetic, the grotesque, forms a particularly important part" of his Appalachian novels.[72] The gothic and grotesque saturate McCarthy's Appalachian work, surely making Cormac McCarthy the godfather of the contemporary Appalachian gothic and his influence on more recent gothic

Appalachian fiction is palpable. To name but a few of those Appalachian authors indebted to McCarthy, William Gay's fiction is commonly compared with McCarthy, an influence Gay acknowledged in several interviews. The landscapes in Gay's fiction are menacing, and from the devastated land and disinterred bodies that make way for a dam in *Provinces of Night* (2000), to the graves exposed by brother and sister Kenneth and Connie Tyler as they discover the macabre actions of the local funeral director, Fenton Breece in *Twilight* (2006), among several literary influences at play in Gay's novels and short stories, McCarthy's is the most keenly detected.

Echoes of McCarthy's Lester Ballard, the necrophiliac murderer and corpse collector in *Child of God* (1973), are discernible in Laura Benedict's *Devil's Oven* (2012), a novel that owes as much to Mary Shelley as to McCarthy, an Appalachian horror that opens with Ivy Luttrell sewing together "the beautiful man whose dismembered body she had found" on the mountain.[73] Ballard's shadows also resonate in David Joy's *The Line that Held Us* (2018) where Dwayne Brewer collects his brother's body and stores the rotting corpse watching it disintegrate as the novel unfolds: "his face grotesque and disfigured [...] Large blisters covered his arms, marbled skin almost glossy [...] His eyes were popping out of his head, his tongue bulging."[74] Dwayne cannot let his brother's corpse go, even when his bloated body collapses "liquefied into an almost creamy consistency, the greenish-black of pond water."[75] Readers of this novel are sure to recall Ballard's body collection and the "Gray soapy clots of matter" and the dripping "gray rheum" that fall from the bodies as the authorities remove them from the cave at the end of *Child of God*.[76] Undoubtedly, McCarthy leaves a lasting legacy on the Appalachian gothic.

The Appalachian gothic, like all forms of the gothic, is richly diverse and in the following chapters I cover some of the most salient and pressing forms of the gothic in contemporary Appalachian literature, in Chapter 1 focusing on war and diseases of despair, in Chapter 2 on extraction and the climate crisis, and in Chapter 3 on race and LGBTQ+ rights. These topics do not cover every aspect of the gothic in Appalachian literature, but I hope that the range of authors and topics I explore provide critical insights into the Appalachian gothic in the late twentieth and twenty-first centuries. The dominant concerns in contemporary Appalachian literature and the gothic forms they take, constitute both a distinct regional voice, yet also deeply connect Appalachia to the nation that continues to other it in the post-Trump moment.

Notes

1 Davenport, "Appalachian Gothic."
2 Robinson, "From The Kallikaks to The Kallikaks," 1.

3 Eller, "Foreword," ix.
4 Vance's highly derogatory discussion of Appalachia and its people resulted in Harkins and McCarroll's edited collection, *Appalachian Reckoning*.
5 Useful starting points for exploring Appalachia's gothic folklore include Nancy Roberts's extensive work on Appalachian hauntings and ghosts, and Patrick W. Gainer's *Witches, Ghosts and Signs*. In literature, Manly Wade Wellman's "Silver John" stories, including *John the Balladeer* (1988), draw on several Appalachian folktales and ballads.
6 There is a vast array of Appalachian fantastic texts that are deeply gothic. These texts include Elizabeth Mazzie's novels, most notably *Sineater* (1994) and *Desper Hollow* (2013). More recently, Shawn Burgess's *The Tear Collector* (2019) and *Ghosts of Grief Hollow* (2022) are further examples of this genre. For a wider discussion of the southern fantastic, see F. Brett Cox and Andy's Duncan's edited book, *Crossroads*.
7 Brown, *Gods of Howl Mountain*, 5–6.
8 Feldman, *Approaching the Fields*, 42.
9 Monnet, "Gothic Matters," 8.
10 Botting, *Gothic*, 5.
11 Batteau, *The Invention of Appalachia*, 15.
12 Klein, *This Changes Everything*, 172–173.
13 Ibid., 310–311.
14 McClanahan, "Earth-world-planet," 635.
15 Ibid., 644.
16 Goddu, *Gothic America*, 2.
17 For a compelling history of Black people in Appalachia since the 1500s, in particular their shared and complex history with the Cherokee, see Perdue, "Red and Black in the Southern Appalachians."
18 Ibid., 3–4.
19 Eller, ix.
20 Straw, "Introduction," 4.
21 Billings, "Once Upon a Time in 'Trumpalachia'," 52.
22 "Population and Age in Appalachia," Appalachian Regional Commission, accessed April 2, 2024, https://www.arc.gov/about-the-appalachian-region/the-chartbook/appalachias-population/.
23 Batteau, 1.
24 Duck, "Undead Genres/Living Locales," 175.
25 Several leading Appalachian scholars have critically debunked ideas of Appalachian otherness. For useful starting points, see Billings and Blee's *The Road to Poverty*; Straw and Blethen's edited collection *High Mountains Rising*; Billings, Norman, and Ledford's edited collection, *Back Talk from Appalachia* and Batteaux's *Appalachia and America*.
26 Billings, 51.
27 Ibid., 52.
28 Maimon, *Twilight in Hazard*, 3.
29 Robertson, "Gothic Appalachian Literature."
30 Castro, *Flight Risk*, 263.
31 McCollum, "Introduction," 5.
32 Monnet, 7.
33 For a wider survey of Appalachian literature, including references to earlier surveys, see Ted Olsen, "Literature." Also, Miller, Hatfield, and Norman's edited collection,

American Vein, offers a series of essays on a wide range of Appalachian authors and texts.
34 Ledford, "A Landscape and a People Set Apart," 48.
35 Ibid., 49.
36 Botting, 4.
37 Ledford, 49.
38 The likely setting of the story is Davis's hometown of Wheeling, West Virginia, an important industrial town on the Ohio River. At the time Davis wrote the story, Wheeling was still part of Virginia.
39 Davis, "Life in the Iron Mills," 2599.
40 Ibid., 2599–2600.
41 Ibid., 2602–2603.
42 For an interesting discussion of the intersections of industry and the environment in Davis's story, see Gatlin, "Disturbing Aesthetics."
43 See Wilson, "A Judicious Combination of Incident and Psychology," for a critical exploration of stereotypes in Fox's fiction.
44 "Trail of the Lonesome Pine: Outdoor Drama," Heart of Appalachia, accessed December 28, 2023, http://www.trailofthelonesomepine.com/drama/.
45 Satterwhite, *Dear Appalachia*, 62–63.
46 Fox Jr. *The Trail of the Lonesome Pine*, chap. 20.
47 McNally, *Monsters of the Market*, 253.
48 McNeill, *Gauley Mountain*, 59.
49 Ibid., 66.
50 Page, *Daughter of the Hills*, 186. It is important to note that while this novel was published in 1950, Page began writing it in the 1930s and it is considered a "novel of the thirties."
51 Wills, "Remembering the Disaster at Hawks Nest."
52 Brown, *Gone Home*, 22.
53 Douglass, "Foreword, Hawk's Nest," ix.
54 Skidmore, *Hawk's Nest*, 266.
55 McNally, 2.
56 Unrue, "The Gothic Matrix of *Look Homeward, Angel*," 48.
57 Wolfe, *Look Homeward, Angel*, 79.
58 For a critical discussion of Wolfe's position as a southern modernist, see Cobb, "Afterword."
59 Evans, *Look Abroad, Angel*.
60 Arnow, *The Dollmaker*, 166.
61 Fraser, *Hillbilly Highway*, 3.
62 Claborn, "From Black Marxism to Industrial Ecosystem," 578–579.
63 Mooney, "Agrarian Tragedy," 34.
64 Turner,
65 Dykeman, *Return the Innocent Earth*, 6.
66 Ibid., 33.
67 Ibid., 373.
68 Ibid., 369.
69 Jones III, "Social Criticism in the Works of Wilma Dykeman," 83.
70 Ibid., 81.
71 Wester, *African American Gothic*, 1.

72 Cooper, "McCarthy, Tennessee, and the Southern Gothic," 41.
73 Benedict, *Devil's Oven*, 1.
74 Joy, *The Line that Held Us*, 113.
75 Ibid., 139.
76 McCarthy, *Child of God*, 196.

Chapter 1

War and Diseases of Despair in Gothic Appalachian Literature

Wars and diseases of despair are neither uniquely Appalachian nor southern nor American, but they are decidedly gothic. As Agnieszka Soltysik Monnet and Steffan Hantke indicate, "The Gothic [...] thrived in its infancy, in times of war" and from "the atrocities of the French Revolution" to "the Napoleonic Wars," warfare "provided a steady background noise to the development of the genre."[1] Moreover, Carol Davison argues that ever since its earliest iterations "the Gothic and addiction go virtually hand-in-glove."[2] While the war gothic and what Davison terms, "Gothic pharmography," cannot be claimed by any one subgenre of the gothic, Appalachia's complex role in the Civil War where many communities held divided loyalties between the Union and Confederacy, its high percentage of military personnel, and the propensity for diseases of despair where poverty and limited job opportunities can result in high addiction levels, mean both the war gothic and gothic pharmography recur across the region's literature.[3] Appalachian authors commonly turn to Civil War ghosts, traumatized war veterans, zombie-like drug addicts, and vampiric Big Pharma, as they present a region that, according to Stephen J. Scanlan, is "'mined' for its citizens in the same way it has been mined for coal," a region highly susceptible to the machinations of Big Pharma and military recruitment.[4]

For Monnet and Hantke, the Civil War gothic largely emerged after 1865,[5] and as Leigh M. McLennon explains, typically, "The history of the Civil War is often framed through narratives that posit binaries about slavery versus freedom, the North versus the South and, correspondingly, good versus evil."[6] However, such binaries do not hold up in many parts of Appalachia. As Kenneth W. Noe notes, one of the many misapprehensions of Appalachia is that the region was almost "totally Unionist," a stereotype "rejected [...] by modern Appalachian historians" who have revealed the region also had a significant Confederate population.[7] At the same time, George McKinney explains, across the region "the majority of mountaineers resisted the move to create a separate Southern nation," a "sentiment" that "was strongest in

East Tennessee, northwestern Virginia, western Maryland, and southeastern Kentucky" where a commitment to the Confederacy was not immediately guaranteed.[8] Indeed, as the war raged on Appalachia witnessed increasing levels of violence between "fluid groupings of Confederate sympathizers, Unionists, and those who rejected both ideologies to avoid the horrors of war."[9] Rebecca Harding Davis captured these fault lines where individuals and communities found themselves on different sides of the conflict.[10] For Noe, Davis "depicts an Appalachia violently at war with itself in a feeding frenzy of murder and retaliation,"[11] as we see in "David Gaunt," where Davis presents a place where the lines between the Union and the Confederacy are not clear-cut.[12] So, while across the South "the Confederacy's demise almost instantaneously gave birth to a Lost Cause ethos that suspiciously bears the marks of undeadness in its symbolic resurrection of fallen C.S.A. hero-saints," Appalachia's relationship to the war is knottier and Civil War undeadness does not always wear the cloak of the Lost Cause.[13]

Yet the Civil War is far from the only war that features repeatedly across Appalachian literature. Scanlan's study of solider deaths in the Iraq War notes that "Appalachia has a significantly higher proportion of the population who are veterans when compared to the rest of the United States," a fact that accounts for the high volume of veterans who appear in the region's literature.[14] Indeed, contemporary Appalachian authors reflect both on the Civil War and subsequent U.S. wars and foreign policy, or what Johan Höglund terms *"American imperial gothic"*. Höglund is particularly interested in the role of the gothic in the period after 9/11, arguing

> the American imperial gothic of recent years maps both the perceived need to aggressively defend, and at times even expand, the ideological and territorial boundaries the United States has established, and the profound anxiety connected to the experience that these borders are, indeed, constantly challenged, that the gothic Other is at the door, and that the apocalypse is imminent.[15]

Several Appalachian authors deploy the gothic as they interrogate U.S. foreign policy and its impacts both at home and abroad, because, as Monnet and Hantke argue "Cutting through the facile certainties and oversimplifications of war propaganda [...] it is first and foremost the Gothic that does justice to our collective fascination with the horror and complexity of war."[16] Appalachian war gothic presents "the horror and complexity of war" in visceral and repeated detail, exploring the inherent challenges for veterans and their families in a region proud of its military service but also victim to predatory recruitment drives that prey on low-income communities.

Moving from the gothic horrors of war, this chapter turns to the ongoing battles against diseases of despair in Appalachia,[17] diseases that result in increased rates of "morbidity and mortality from three main causes—alcohol, prescription drug and illegal drug overdose; suicide; and alcoholic liver disease/cirrhosis of the liver."[18] While diseases of despair are prolific in communities across the United States, in a 2019 study Michael Meit, Megan Heffernan, and Erin Tanenbaum found that "When comparing Appalachia to the non-Appalachian U.S., the most notable disparities in overdose deaths existed for the group 25–44 years. Young adults in Appalachia are considerably more likely to die from an overdose than similar-aged adults in the rest of the U.S."[19] Contemporary Appalachian literature grapples with these drug crises, often depending on traditional gothic forms including zombies and vampires as authors seek to go beyond statistics.

Yet, in their discussion of the use of extreme images in anti-meth, public health campaigns, Witney Marsh, Heith Copes and Travis Linnemann, are concerned that the presentation of "methamphetamine users" as "diseased, zombie-like White trash" are "drawn from pre-existing understandings of the rural poor as uneducated, degenerate, atavistic throwbacks."[20] Certainly, in Appalachian gothic pharmography there is always the risk that focusing on the horrors of addicts' bodily disintegration may offer little more than a tableau of Appalachian otherness, and Billings cautions against pathologizing "Appalachain traits—drug addiction, teen pregnancy and illegitimacy, violence, fatalism, the lack of a work ethic, 'learned helplessness,' poverty as a 'family tradition,' the inability to face the truth about one's self, and so on." While the region's authors illustrate the myriad of problems that arise in relation to addiction, they perhaps do not always offer a more balanced insight into "the region's grassroots struggles to build a post-coal economy, nor its past and ongoing struggles for economic, labor, environmental, and social justice."[21] However, their gothic turns to the broken bodies of drug crises typically offer nuanced insights that take readers beyond mere spectacle to understand the wider socioeconomic and political forces behind addiction. Rather than merely providing narratives of ruin, Appalachian gothic pharmography explores addiction with empathy, even in texts where the brutality and costs of addiction are laid bare.[22] So, from the Civil War to drug crises, this chapter turns to a range of contemporary authors who represent the multifarious, gothic nature of war, from battlefields to meth houses.

War and Appalachian Gothic Literature

The often bitter divides between Union and Confederate loyalty in Appalachia means the Civil War undead in its literature complicate the North/South divide and in Sharyn McCrumb's *Ghost Riders* (2003),[23] and Ron Rash's *The World Made Straight* (2006), the Shelton Laurel massacre looms large, a massacre that was a particularly dark blight in Appalachia's Civil War story.[24] Indeed, John C. Inscoe and Gordon B. McKinney highlight the Shelton Laurel massacre as an event that "came to define the new terms under which the war would be waged in the mountains."[25] From this point on, guerilla war tactics were deployed in parts of Appalachia, tactics that "blurred the lines between combatants and noncombatants and obscured the rules of war that defined both."[26] In Rash's novel all Travis Shelton knows about the war is that "Sometimes my Daddy and uncle talked about kin that got killed in Shelton Laurel during the war, but I always figured the Yankees had done it."[27] Under the tutelage of Leonard Schuler, and excerpts from the diary of Leonard's great-great-grandfather, a Civil War doctor, Travis learns that Confederate soldiers of the North Carolina 64th regiment were responsible for violently killing his relatives.

Leonard contemplates the treatment of the dead that "implied something more than mere retribution. A sergeant had danced on the bodies when they'd been dumped in a ditch, vowing to push them into hell. By the time the kin had gotten to the meadow, wild hogs had eaten one man's head off."[28] Rash reflects on these violent deaths and their haunting traces not only in the novel but also in his poem "Shelton Laurel: 2006" (2008)[29] where he focuses on the body of 13-year-old David Shelton, one of the victims who had pleaded "not to be shot."[30] McCrumb writes too of the Shelton boy, his screams and how one "of the bullets hit Davey in the face, and he fell forward [...] then he lay still in the red-streaked snow."[31] These murders constitute a war crime that in Rash's poem is seared into the earth, turning the land into "a palimpsest" that carries the traces of the dead, their graves lying beneath the "shadows" cast over the sowed earth.[32]

In McCrumb's *Ghost Riders* and Ann Pancake's "Ghostless" (2001), the Civil War dead are restless, rising out of the troubled earth. In McCumb's novel, echoes of "the old days" become manifest,[33] not only in the Civil War reenactments that refuse to "turn loose of that war," but also the ghost riders who cannot rest.[34] In Pancake's story, the narrator, looking back on his childhood in Appalachia, remembers it is a place "thick with ghosts."[35] He, and his "Ghost-dogged" daddy regularly saw apparitions,[36] from old timers "clambering empty-handed up the banks and always fading back into the dead leaves" to "Confederates, again and again, the Confederates, all the time watching the ground under their feet."[37] These Confederate ghosts fixate on the earth, seemingly trapped there in perpetuity. Daniel Cross Turner asks, "Why does the Confederacy rise again and again—unfulfilled—in ghostly forms? Does their ghostliness mask or unveil deeper cultural fault lines, confirm or deny official historiographies of the war and its continuing aftermaths?"[38] In Pancake's story Confederate ghosts are locked to the land, caught in limbo between the Civil War and the world that emerged in its wake, mirroring the struggle of the narrator's father who cannot reconcile the impending loss of his family's old homeplace.

This story is both about the ghosts of the past that wander around because *"there's nowhere else for them to go"* and the ghost-dogged father who sees his own hopelessness in theirs. With the old family home foreclosed, now "a ghost itself" sagging and "vine-swallowed" and swamped by the second homes that grow like some form of voracious monster that grows larger and larger, squeezing everything else out, the father takes his own life, choosing, perhaps, to join the ghosts rather than face the reality of being pushed off the land.[39] Pancake writes across her fiction about the horrors that come with out-of-towners buying up land and building second homes, but in this story she utilizes Confederate ghosts to explore the costs of being unable or unwilling to change. Although his son laments the loss of their rural home from the city where "it is all straights and angles, your eye broken up by corners and by edges," at the very least he is not trapped on that land, wandering around and around with Confederate ghosts and his father, trapped in an idea of place.[40]

Reflecting on the haunting vestiges of the Civil War, Kentucky native bell hooks situates the war alongside several horrors of the past, including the removal and genocide of Indigenous people, slavery and segregation in her poetry collection *Appalachian Elegy* (2012) where, in poem 45 she reflects on the many ghosts who "gather here."[41] In echoes of Effie Waller Smith's poem "The Lone Grave on the Mountain" in her 1904 collection *Song of the Months*, hooks calls for acknowledging the past but not being trapped by it. Waller Smith, a Black poet at the start of the twentieth century, wrote a significant number of poems and three short stories in her early life, many of which focus on her Kentucky birthplace. In Waller Smith's poem, the speaker laments the Confederate soldier's "solitary grave" on Bull Mountain, Kentucky, and the knowledge that his family knows "not where he reposes." Waller Smith requests kindness and "love" for the "dust of the sleeping soldier," asking, "Can't we forgive his fault?/And the faults of fellow soldiers/As we stand by his wooden vault?" The poem does not dispense with fault, but Waller Smith's faith demands that the unnamed solider in his "lonely spot" be saved, a call to prevent him from becoming one of the restless Confederate ghosts that feature in Appalachian literature.[42] Over a hundred years later, so much rests on the opening line of hooks's poem 51, where "in the gray blue wash of dawn" the colors that demarcated Confederates and Unionists merge, the two bitterly opposed sides subtly fused in the morning light.[43] In poem 51 hooks draws hope from the ability of the land to renew, a form of renewal that might alleviate the horrors of war and reinstate a sense of shared humanity "beyond country flag nation."[44] Yet wars of the past are only part of the problem with Appalachian fiction replete with the ghosts and hauntings of U.S. foreign policy since the Civil War, author after author capturing the brutality of conflict on those at home and abroad, authors including Jayne Anne Phillips, Marie Manilla, Taylor Brown, David Joy, and Ron Rash, to name but a few.

In his novels *Potted Meat* (2016) and *Water and Power* (2018), both experimental novels that combine poetry and prose, West Virginian and Black U.S. Navy veteran-turned-author, Steven Dunn, reflects at length about military recruitment and service after 9/11. In *Potted Meat*, his narrator recalls growing up in a Black community in a small town and the ways military recruiters prey on poor Black people scarred and shaped by alcoholism, domestic and child abuse, and racism. The novel is composed of a series of vignettes in which the narrator discusses his young life and his aspirations, sharing his desire to "be an architect, godammit."[45] Yet in the very next vignette, he explains that his "cousin joined the Navy" and his "recruiter comes to our school all the time and flirts with the girls and the boys."[46] Despite the rapacious recruiter, the narrator holds firm to his convictions about attending college, but when his sister goes to college only to return home early "because something happened to her at that big university in Ohio," the family loses its desire to support their son's college dream.[47] In the next vignette the narrator reveals, "I joined the Navy. So did Leonard and Dee."[48] The fast, unrelenting pace of this novel highlights a life trapped by circumstances. Dunn makes clear, joining the Navy was a choice in name only, and his narrator joins the Navy in 1999 only because he is reassured by the recruiter that "there wont be another war until after long youre retired," but, of course, 9/11 changes everything.

Dunn follows his narrator into military service in *Water & Power*, a novel that includes Dunn's accounts of interviews with people in or connected to the U.S. military that capture pride, disappointment, and hate toward military service. This experimental novel also draws on documents and images, and at the end, Dunn inserts a 23-page list of civilians killed in Iraq, Pakistan, and Afghanistan drawn from The Bureau of Investigative Journalism to underscore his wider critique of collateral damage. While that list focuses on foreign civilians, the novel shows how U.S. military personnel can also become victims of collateral damage. In a deeply gothic and satirical part of the novel, the narrator discusses how he "volunteered to work at the Taxidermy Museum of Military Heroes."[49] In this museum, dead soldiers are taxidermied to be displayed in action scenes, such as the taxidermied soldier in the atrium: "He crouches in shooting position, stuffed white fingers curled around rifle trigger, one eye squints, the other eyeball stares straight ahead."[50] The horrors unfold as the narrator is shown around the museum, including the bodies "ready to be mounted," with their hanging flesh "rounded at the bottom like shirttails" and the "Droopy black holes where eyes once were."[51] While their initial deaths were a horrific outcome of war, the perverse taxidermy process renders them truly monstrous and destined to be frozen in time in a state of animated warfare.

Readers later learn that the sheer number of U.S. soldier deaths means Arlington National Cemetery is full, but "a White House Public Relations Official" reassures everyone that "there are still options for our fallen to be in Arlington" because "there are plans to open five more Taxidermy Museums within the next ten years."[52] In these museums, "Thank you for your service" takes on a darker side. In Dunn's searing account of military life, recruits are potted meat, ready to be shaped and reshaped, even in death. Even those who do survive are left profoundly haunted, with one veteran no longer able to eat meat after his "best friend stepped on a land mine" and "Blood and bits of flesh splattered us. Some even flew into my mouth."[53] Dunn's novel exposes military harm in all its manifestations, with its particular focus on U.S. soldiers and foreign civilians during the Iraq and Afghan wars.

The same conflicts feature in Mark Powell's *The Dark Corner* (2012), where the ghost of a young Iraqi boy haunts Malcolm Walker, a one-time Episcopal priest who returns to his South Carolina home after attempting suicide as a form of protest against the Iraq war in his New England church.[54] The Iraqi boy bares all the scars of geopolitical warfare writ large, and I quote at length to capture the brutality wrought upon the child's body:

> He was […] perhaps six or seven, and judging from his pallor Malcolm guessed he had been dead months before his arrival. His right arm disappeared just above the elbow, though he was always careful to cover the upper humerus with his torn sleeve. His nose was obliterated and a flap of skin covered the socket of the eye he had lost, but it was the textured skin that drew Malcolm. Pockmarked with bits of shrapnel and soft as overripe fruit, it was a pattern of square bulges, perfectly symmetrical, as if he had spent the better part of his childhood pressed against a window screen. When he had failed to speak Malcolm had done some research and found his injuries consistent with those of a cluster bomb. The bomblets were yellow and shiny. Children often picked them up, thinking them toys.[55]

The visceral, detailed description accentuates the full horror of contemporary warfare, of Höglund's "American imperial gothic" and its impact on civilians of all ages. Each detail forms a central part of Powell's wider critique of war and its costs, both in this novel and in his later novels, *The Sheltering* (2014), *Small Treasons* (2017), and *The Late Rebellion* (2024). In this novel, that critique is particularly stark: Powell's decision to include the child ghost with all his fatal injuries exposes the realities of collateral damage. Similarly, Nikki Giovanni, an outspoken critic of the Vietnam War, a war she railed against in much of her poetry in the 1960s and early 1970s, worries in "Atrocities" about what it means to live "in age of napalmed children."[56] Decades later, Powell asks similar questions in *The Dark Corner* where the boy, who draws Malcolm's attention to "the great online cache of the Abu Ghraib photographs, a single website composed wholly of suffering," is a constant reminder of American war atrocities.[57] After attempting suicide in his church as a mark of protest against the Iraq War, Malcolm is committed to a psychiatric ward where he makes a second suicide attempt when he is led by the boy to a supply closet where he finds and drinks a "gallon of antifreeze."[58]

Powell follows the opening section detailing the boy's appearance and Malcolm's mental health crisis with an opening chapter dwelling on the ongoing trauma and flashbacks that plague Malcolm's father, Elijah, a Vietnam War veteran. Elijah recalls trying to drown out his memories with alcohol, but he could never shake the images of the "dead paratroopers" or the "VC curled fetally, burnt out of tunnels by demo teams, charred until they were nothing but zippers and the melted eyelets of boots," their bodies vaporized, leaving only the material traces of their existence.[59] Alongside his psychological torment, Elijah is also in acute physical pain, but the grisly discovery of his "strangely distended abdomen" only occurs after a tractor accident.[60] At the moment of the accident, Elijah is overwrought by memories, the past and the present combining in horrid unison as the tree line in front of him becomes a battlefield hot zone, with "men falling without sound, crumpling, the chaos of crawling. The dead like dancers in their awkward poses, pretzeled in the mud," a grotesque performance in the midst of war.[61] Powell's veterans, like so many across Appalachian literature, live with these agonizing memories, and in *The Dark Corner* the ghost of the Iraqi boy is a haunting reminder of collateral damage and the number of innocent lives sacrificed in war. Given Malcolm's mental health problems, the ghost may, of course, be a figment of his imagination, but given Powell's wider exploration of war, foreign policy, and geopolitics across his writing, it matters not whether Malcolm imagines the ghost or whether the boy is an actual apparition, his place in the novel is a haunting reminder of the uncanny nature of warfare that is a dominant strain in Appalachian literature.

Covering a very different but no less important aspect of U.S. military service, Affrilachian poet Nikky Finney writes powerfully in "Florissant" about Private First Class LaVena Johnson's brutal death in Iraq in 2005,[62] a poem that "has now been entered into the Congressional Record of the United States of America in the name of thousands of women enlisted and assaulted in the U.S. Armed Services."[63] The haunting poem viscerally recounts the violence inflicted on Johnson's body despite the Department for Defense ruling her death a suicide. Finney ends the poem with a call for readers to repeat and therefore remember that women in the U.S. military have "*a higher chance of being raped by a fellow soldier/than being killed by enemy fire.*"[64] While startling statistics lay bare unpalatable truths, Finney's poem pushes beyond statistics, confronting readers as she juxtaposes Johnson's hopes and ambitions with the dehumanizing brutality of her death. Sexual violence in the military also features heavily in Dunn's *Water & Power* where Dunn offers a detailed account of the Tailhook Scandal and the ways the military continues to cover up sexual violence.

From the worst of modern warfare all the way back not just to the Civil War but also to the forced removal and genocide of Indigenous people to which I turn in Chapter 3, Appalachian literature is a space where military service and its costs are critically interrogated. So, despite J. D. Vance's suggestion in *Hillbilly Elegy* that military service is exactly what unemployed "food stamp recipients" in Appalachia require, the region's authors repeatedly, and via gothic tropes, present the costs of military service, both physically and mentally, and at home and abroad.[65]

If war and warfare are defining features of the Appalachian gothic, then so too are the battles waged against diseases of despair with a significant number of contemporary Appalachian writers turning to the devastating impacts of addiction and the predatory machinations of Big Pharma and illegal drug dealers. In their collaborative poetry collection, *Specter Mountain* (2018), Jesse Graves and William Wright contemplate in "Mother" about the many pollutants destroying the biosphere, and alongside common culprits including farming run-off and industry pollution, the natural world in this poem also bears the scars of diseases of despair, from strains of "benzodiazepine" to "runoff from a meth house."[66] Impacting the human and non-human, diseases of despair form an ongoing, ever-present war across Appalachian communities.

Diseases of Despair and the Appalachian Gothic

It is common across recent Appalachian fiction for its gothic monsters and demons to emerge out of diseases of despair and the opioid, meth, and heroin crises. These crises give substance to the contemporary rural noir where authors often explore the dark, violent side of the drug trade and to realist texts that dwell on the horrors of addiction. In this section, I consider both approaches and their contribution to the Appalachian gothic. In David Joy's novel, *When These Mountains Burn* (2020), Raymond Mathis importantly recognizes that the waves of drug crises that have blighted Appalachia are not a regional problem but "an American problem. That was escapist cure for systemic poverty, the result of putting profit margins ahead of people for two hundred years," a system only exacerbated by Trump despite his repeated overtures to the poor.[67] Travis Linneman and Corina Medley underscore that "the Trump administration's response to the opioid problem […] powerfully articulates the cynical resignation to 'business as usual' that characterizes capitalist realism," a realism that continues to produce attendant horrors.[68] Certainly, as Meit, Heffernan and Tanenbaum indicate, "Over the past two decades, mortality from overdose, suicide, and alcoholic liver diseases/cirrhosis has increased across the US," but as they also highlight "the disparity between Appalachian and the non-Appalachian US continues to grow."[69] The unnaturalness of so many young deaths across Appalachia is horrifying, and something that haunts deputy sheriff, Johnny Boy, in Chris Offutt's recent series of crime novels:[70] *The Killing Hills* (2021),[71] *Shifty's Boys* (2022),[72] and *Code of the Hills* (2023)[73] that follow Mick Hardin, a complex, brooding combat veteran and Army CID agent who finds himself back home in "the shadowed land" of eastern Kentucky on multiple sojourns where he works with his sister, Linda, the local Sheriff, to solve crimes often relating to the devastating impacts of the illegal drug trade operating both in and beyond Kentucky's state lines.[74] While Offutt trades on a sense of Appalachian otherness or at least distinctiveness with his emphasis across these novels on the ways Appalachians continue to live "by old codes" shaped by personal vengeance, he also portrays a place devastated by extractive industries and the drug trade.[75]

Offutt turns to both deforestation and life expectancy levels in *The Killing Hills*, where Johnny Boy is preoccupied by the lower life expectancy levels in Appalachia than other parts of the United States, telling Linda "Everywhere else, folks live a bit longer every year. Our lives are getting shorter on average."[76] Johnny's fears are palpable, and in his wider work on haunting and monsters, Leo Braudy asks "What makes us afraid?"[77] Interestingly, in this novel the answer lies in the horror of living in a region where lives are abnormally cut short. In her work on death and the gothic, Davison argues that Mary Shelley's *Frankenstein* "makes eminently clear that we all, as Victor's literal walking corpse reminds us, carry our future corpse within us: all who live must, inevitably die."[78] Yet this knowledge is amplified for those living in communities where life expectancy rates are markedly lower than the national average. Interestingly, while Johnny Boy is terrified about life expectancy rates, he struggles to locate the exact cause. His fear is at once acute and misplaced: he has an irrational fear of funeral homes because "He's afraid of ghosts"[79] and he claims that "The hills are killing us."[80] The Appalachian woods, like woods and forests in many cultures, are often regarded as primal gothic sites. As Elizabeth Parker outlines, "The Gothic forest—that is, the frightening and foreboding forest—is an archetypal site of dread in the collective human imagination," yet Offutt shows across the Mick Hardin novels that people rather than the hills pose the greatest threat.[81]

For Offutt, the devastating impacts of the drug trade from opioids through to heroin and meth pose a significant threat to individuals and communities in Kentucky. In *The Code of the Hills*, Mick encounters Charley Flowers, a Detroit drug dealer who, after the "crackdown on OxyContin in the hills [...] filled the market demand by utilizing the old 'hillbilly highway' to move smack into Appalachia," a seemingly never-ending array of addictive substances pumped into economically depressed communities.[82] While her brother works in the shady world of drug producers and distributors, in *The Killing Hills*, Linda encounters the direct impact of that trade on addicts when she attends the scene of a car crash and quickly recognizes that the victims are part of the opioid crisis. As she looks around the car before the State Police arrive, Linda takes a metal inventory which lays the horror bare: "Three empty packs of cigarettes, a lighter, a packet of ketchup, four stale French fries, and a corpse."[83] The location of the addict's body at the end of this list highlights both its starkness and its everydayness: another victim of a merciless drug trade. Offutt's primary interest across the Hardin novels is the production and distribution of illegal drugs in and beyond Kentucky, an interest that also recurs through the novels of fellow Appalachian noir writers, Brian Panowich, David Joy, and Ron Rash.[84]

Take Rash's short story, "Those Who Are Dead Are Only Now Forgiven" (2003), that explores the impact of the meth crisis on young Appalachians. In the story, meth producers and addicts Lauren, Katie Lynn and Billy inhabit the story's haunted house, a house where "locals heard the whispered misery of ghosts. Footsteps creaked on stair boards and sobs filtered through the walls."[85] This traditional gothic space is a fitting venue for new horrors. Central to the story is Jody, a college student and Lauren's childhood sweetheart. Jody tracks down Lauren at the haunted house and on arrival notices how the "odor of meth singed the air."[86] On witnessing the profound physical changes in the three, "Jody imagined a breed of meth heads evolving to veins and nose and mouth, just enough flesh on bone to keep the passageways open."[87] Seeing their zombified state, Jody touches Lauren's hand and discovers it "was warm, blood still pulsing through it yet," relieved that she is not yet lost but fully cognizant of the dramatic changes wrought upon her body.[88] However, the gothic strains in Rash's story are neither restricted to the meth-head zombies living in the haunted house, nor the wider community's insularity, but also extend to the deformed hands of Jody's mother and sister who carry the physical pains and scars of working in a poultry plant, and to the massive burden of student debt that plagues Jody.[89]

The story is infected by a sense of despair and the idea of fate versus choice is played out in the story's twist that sees Jody relinquishing his studies for the meth life. On entering the haunted house at the end of the story, and after one final and failed attempt to coerce Lauren away from meth, he places his money "in the collection plate," the church collection plate where Lauren, Katie Lynn, and Billie keep spare change and meth paraphernalia.[90] The plate acts as the nexus of faith, money and meth, and making his offering, Jody commits himself to a new life order. While this meth community believes it saves him, Jody knows better. Theirs is a death-in-life existence, but with his other path filled with overwhelming financial obstacles if he is to escape the menial or injurious jobs available in Haywood, in the end, he embraces overt zombification over blind zombification. Jody makes a potentially fatal decision, or what Davison might term a "fatal exchange," but one that he makes fully cognizant of the outcome.[91] In his study of necroculture and capitalism, Charles Thorpe argues that the "pleasure in being a zombie is the pleasure of escape from a humanness that has become alien."[92] In the end, the price for fighting against the odds and making it through college with "the debilitating weight of student loan debt" is a burden, or form of alienation, that Jody relinquishes.[93] In their work on "drug writers" Jayson Althofer and Brian Musgrove indicate, the "'horror' of addiction is imbricated with the horrified recoil from mass modernity," one horror substituted with another, something frequently represented across addiction literature.[94]

Robert Brinkmeyer surmises that readers leave Rash's story haunted, forced "to ponder the fundamental values by which we guide our lives." For Brinkmeyer, Jody's decision rests on "a mysterious, dangerous, and appealing irrationality" that haunts even the most rational, but the move to inner desires and psychology forgoes Rash's gothic exposure of the irrational demands and abuses of neoliberalism.[95] Readers certainly leave this story haunted, but it haunts not only in what it uncovers about hidden human desires, but what it reveals about imprisoning socioeconomic factors that hamper the lives of characters across gothic Appalachian fiction. As Monnet outlines,

> Among the most compelling of quotidian horrors to have emerged in recent decades is a world shaped by neoliberal economies and social philosophy. Many scholars believe that it is no accident that the Gothic has emerged so forcefully at precisely the same moment, and has provided a repertoire of images, tropes and monsters that both reflect and critically explore this new global order.[96]

Jody may choose the monstrosity of addiction, but in so doing he relinquishes the challenges posed by "this new global order."

In an equally powerful and devastating short story, "Kittens" (2023), Megan Lucas, a Canadian-born author now residing in North Carolina, exposes the demonic force of addiction that sucks the life out of an addict's family. The story follows Cheryl, a wife and mother of four children, the eldest of whom, Hannah, is an addict who dies at the start of the narrative. Cheryl and her husband, Tim, desperately tried to save their daughter, paying for costly rehab, but at the end of the story, Lucas reveals the horror-filled truth that Cheryl deliberately left Hannah unattended with the somber expectation that she would overdose. Cheryl is forced to make this brutal decision to save her remaining family because "Waiting to save Hannah was killing them."[97] Cheryl recognizes that "the fallout of addiction was financially devastating," but worse, and in vampiric fashion, Hannah's addiction drains her family and Cheryl forfeits Hannah to save her remaining children.[98]

The complex representations of addiction across Appalachian literature are deeply gothic, painfully complex, and take readers into worlds of acute suffering where answers are never straightforward. Indeed, in Frank X Walker's deeply autobiographical *About Flight* (2015), a collection of poems about his brother's addiction, he writes agonizingly about the love and anger he felt as his brother deteriorated when he descended into addiction after returning from military service. He writes in "Paratrooper," "When Brother comes down from a high/he moves like a ghost trapped on the ground," every time a little bit less like himself.[99] From those Appalachian noir novels that expose the machinations of the drug trade to the realist texts that explore the devastating costs drug crises have on individuals, families and communities, Appalachian gothic pharmography is brutal and necessary.

While texts including those of Rash, Lucas and Walker dwell largely on cycles of relapse and hopelessness, Barbara Kingsolver's *Demon Copperhead* (2022) powerfully illustrates both the devastating impacts of addiction and the avenues for recovery. In a novel influenced by Charles Dickens's *David Copperfield* (1850), central protagonist and first-person narrator Damon Fields, better known as Demon Copperhead, charts his journey from birth to adulthood, a journey pitted by poverty, addiction, violence, death, despair, and ultimately hope. Kingsolver tackles the horrifying rates of morbidity and mortality among the young through Demon's journey through the foster system, a journey set in motion after his mother, a long-time addict, undergoes rehab before succumbing to a deadly overdose.

For all the horrors he experiences throughout his young life, the period when he feels his humanity slipping away most acutely comes when he is prescribed opioids after suffering a football injury. Demon's addiction is fueled by his unhealthy romantic relationship with Dori who supplies them with her dying father's medication, and who tragically dies despite Demon's best efforts to help her. Demon recognizes his loss of humanity during his extensive period of addiction, detailing the emotions of "staving off the dopesickness" with Dori:[100] "Empty, you are a monster. The person you love is monstrous."[101] Narrating his life during recovery, Demon reflects on this period when opioids totally controlled his life, and in Kingsolver's calculations, if opioids make addicts feel and often appear monstrous, then Purdue Pharma is a contemporary Frankenstein. Demon is largely saved from his monstrous state by June, the aunt of his childhood friend, Maggot. Aunt June, a medic who experiences the fallout of the opioid crisis first-hand and briefly dates a Purdue rep, helps Demon to recognize big pharma as a predator.[102] While in *Hillbilly Elegy* Vance refuses to acknowledge that "governments or corporations or anyone else" should be held accountable for aspects of drug crises, Kingsolver and fellow Appalachian authors refuse to simply pathologize individuals, exposing the wider systems that actively encourage addiction.[103]

Demon's schoolteacher Mr. Armstrong also educates Demon on the true monstrosity at the heart of his life. In one moment where Demon reflects on the Appalachian history he learns from Mr. Armstrong, he thinks about the deep attachment to the coal industry in Appalachia, an attachment that is difficult to break. Demon realizes how vampiric, capitalist, extractive forces have drained Appalachia's land and its people, leaving "war wounds" that will not heal: mountain tops that will not regrow and rivers that will not miraculously recover from the runoff and other pollutants that destroy biodiversity. Images of mountain tops "blown off" and "rivers running black" sit firmly in both the gothic and realist realms, at once deeply uncanny yet all too real.[104] After all, as Tom Butler and George Wuerthner outline, "According to government figures for 2005, more than 1.8 billion pounds of high explosives were used in West Virginia and Kentucky alone, primarily in surface-mining operations,"[105] the land violently exploded and viewed as necessary collateral damage to keep the lights on. If Mr. Armstrong helps Demon to conceptualize the causes of despair, then both at work and at home, June strives tirelessly to help the victims of the opioid crisis and her unrelenting hope saves her family members, Emmy and Maggot, as well as Demon, from the path of addiction.[106]

Even when Demon is in recovery and pursuing an artistic career, his new path is heavily shaped by his formative, horror-filled journey, especially his experiences in the foster care system where he suffers neglect and hunger, including at the first foster house, Mr. Crickson's farm, where the children are poorly fed and used as free labor. It is a stark entry into foster life for Demon, but the friendship he develops with Tommy Waddles becomes one of the lynchpin relationships in Demon's life.[107] During his recovery, Tommy inspires Demon to create a series of drawings based on the superhero, Neckbones, a character Demon first conjured at the Crickson foster home where he was influenced by the skeletons young Tommy constantly drew after losing his parents.

Given Demon's experiences, and the regional knowledge he gains from Tommy and Mr. Armstrong, it is fitting that he writes Appalachian history "through the eyes of skeletons."[108] His strip includes a focus on extractive disasters such as the 1959 Knox Mine Disaster in Pennsylvania and "a strip about a junkie couple trying to keep house" based on his own atypical attempts to establish a home with Dori.[109] Reflecting on why he writes, he remembers something he learned from Mr. Armstrong: "a good story doesn't just copy life, it pushes back on it," which is what Kingsolver does throughout her Appalachian novels, as she writes back against the continued misperceptions of the region.[110] *Demon Copperhead* pushes back in part because Demon's story transcends victimhood. Characters including Mr. Armstrong, Aunt June, and Tommy, all contribute to Demon finding a way out of cyclical addiction and into a career where he tells the tale of his region and its people with humanity and nuance.

Kingsolver's novel is about demons and it is replete with gothic tropes, but Kingsolver refuses to let darkness reign, pushing back again Vance's ruin narrative that posits Appalachia as "a hub of misery."[111] *Demon Copperhead* has its fair share of misery but ruin is only part of the story. At the end of the novel, Demon, Maggot and Emmy are all adjusting to life post-addiction with their individual fates less than certain, but through different means and with differing degrees of agency, they each begin to reclaim their lives. Yet the Appalachian gothic shows that overcoming one obstacle is often never enough in a region where hauntings and monsters take several aggressive forms, and in Chapter 2 I turn to the impacts of extraction and the climate crisis, concerns that run throughout Kingsolver's Appalachian novels as they do across the work of so many of the region's authors and poets.

Notes

1 Monnet and Hantke, "Ghosts from the Battlefields," xi.
2 Davison, "The Gothic and Addiction," 1.
3 Davison, "'Houses of Voluntary Bondage'," 68–85.
4 Scanlan, "'Mined' for Its Citizens?" 47.
5 Monnet and Hantke, xv.
6 McLennon, "'The Red Thirst is on this Nation'," 5.
7 Noe, "'Deadened Color and Colder Horror'," 67.
8 McKinney, "The Civil War and Reconstruction," 46.

9. Ibid., 68.
10. Ibid., 46.
11. Noe, 73.
12. Davis, "David Gaunt," Kindle.
13. Anderson, Hagood, and Turner, "Introduction," 2.
14. Scanlan, 56.
15. Höglund, *The American Imperial Gothic*, 3.
16. Monnet and Hantke, xxiv.
17. For their detailed discussion about deaths of despair, see: Case and Deaton, *Deaths of Despair and the Future of Capitalism*.
18. Meit, Heffernan, and Tanenbaum, "Investigating the Impact of Diseases of Despair in Appalachia," 9.
19. Ibid., 16.
20. Marsh, Copes, and Linnemann, "Creating Visual Differences: Methamphetamine Users Perceptions of Anti-meth Campaigns," 52–53.
21. Billings, "Once Upon a Time in Appalachia," 39.
22. For a detailed study of narratives of ruin and resilience in southern literature, see Spoth, *Ruin and Resilience*.
23. McCrumb, *Ghost Riders*, 4.
24. Rash, *The World Made Straight*.
25. Inscoe and McKinney, *The Heart of Confederate Appalachia*, 117.
26. Ibid. 119.
27. Rash, *The World Made Straight*, 29.
28. Ibid., 206.
29. Rash returns to the Shelton Laurel massacre in his highly satirical short story, "Dead Confederates" in *Burning Bright*, where a plan to steal collectibles from Confederate graves also provides a searing critique of contemporary poverty and the oppressive weight of medical bills.
30. Rash, "Shelton Laurel," 145.
31. McCrumb, 218.
32. Rash, "Shelton Laurel," 145.
33. McCrumb, 2.
34. Ibid., 4.
35. Pancake, *Given Ground*, 3.
36. Ibid., 5.
37. Ibid., 7.
38. Turner, "Gray Ghosts," 62.
39. Pancake, 7.
40. Ibid., 11.
41. hooks, bell, *Appalachian Elegy: Poetry and Place*, 55. Copyright © 2012 Gloria Jean Watkins (bell hooks). Reprinted by permission of The University Press of Kentucky.
42. Waller Smith, *The Collected Works of Effie Waller Smith*, 50–51.
43. Ibid., 61.
44. Ibid.
45. Dunn, *Potted Meat*, 87.
46. Ibid., 88.
47. Ibid., 89.

48 Ibid., 90.
49 Dunn, *Water & Power*, 72.
50 Ibid., 72.
51 Ibid., 78.
52 Ibid., 131.
53 Ibid., 129.
54 Powell, *The Dark Corner*.
55 Ibid., 3.
56 Giovanni, *The Collected Poetry of Nikki Giovanni*, 3407. Kindle.
57 Powell, 5.
58 Ibid., 7.
59 Ibid., 11.
60 Ibid., 186.
61 Ibid., 183.
62 For an overview of LaVena Johnson's death and her parents' campaign for justice, see: "Say Their Names: Green Library Exhibit supporting the Black Lives Matter movement," Stanford Libraries, accessed April 3, 2024, https://exhibits.stanford.edu/saytheirnames/feature/lavena-johnson.
63 Finney, *Love Child's Hotbed of Occasional Poetry*, 195.
64 Ibid., 198.
65 Vance, *Hillbilly Elegy*, 21.
66 Graves and Wright, *Specter Mountain: Poems*, 60.
67 Joy, *When These Mountains Burn*, 251–252.
68 Linneman and Medley, "Down and Out in Middleton and Jackson," 150.
69 Meit, Heffernan, and Tanenbaum, 15.
70 While I focus here on Offutt's recent crime series, his earlier fiction is also deeply gothic. Offutt took a break from writing and started again with *Country Dark* (2018) before starting the Mick Hardin series.
71 Offutt, *The Killing Hills*, 118.
72 Offutt, *Shifty's Boys*.
73 Offutt, *Code of the Hills*.
74 Offutt, *The Killing Hills*, 118.
75 Ibid., 188.
76 Ibid., 48.
77 Braudy, *Haunted*, 1.
78 Davison, "Introduction – The Corpse in the Closet: The Gothic, Death, and Modernity," 4.
79 Offutt, *The Killing Hills*, 53.
80 Ibid., 48.
81 Parker, *The Forest and the EcoGothic*, 1.
82 Offutt, *The Code of the Hills*, 160.
83 Offutt, *The Killing Hills*, 132.
84 Offutt, Panowich and Joy's fiction also sits neatly under the terms "Grit Lit," "Rough South," and "Rural Noir."
85 Rash, *Nothing Gold Can Stay*, 127.
86 Ibid., 130.
87 Ibid., 133.

88 Ibid., 134.
89 For an interesting discussion of "Those Who Are Dead Are Only Now Forgiven" and the tensions around education in Appalachia, see: Presley, "Reconciling Literacy and Loss in Ron Rash's *Nothing Gold Can Stay*."
90 Rash, *Nothing Gold Can Stay*, 143.
91 Davison, "'Houses of Voluntary Bondage'," 70.
92 Thorpe, *Necroculture*, 30.
93 Ibid., 16.
94 Althofer and Musgrove, "'A Ghost in Daylight'," 2.
95 Brinkmeyer, Jr., "Discovering Gold in the Back of Beyond," 221.
96 Monnet, "Gothic Matters," 10.
97 Lucas, *Here in the Dark*, 70.
98 Ibid., 70.
99 Walker, *About Flight*, 7.
100 Kingsolver, *Demon Copperhead*, 408.
101 Ibid., 409.
102 In "Frankenstein and an Empire of Pain," a 2021 review of Patrick Radden Keefe's *Empire of Pain*, an expose of the rise and fall of Purdue Pharma, the Sackler family, and their production and distribution of OxyContin, Sally Haldorson also draws comparisons between big pharma, the opioid crisis, and Mary Shelley's *Frankenstein*. At the time of writing, nitazenes, or so-called "Frankenstein opioids," are the basis of the latest opioid crisis.
103 Vance, 256.
104 Kingsolver, 280.
105 Butler and Wuerthner, ed. *Plundering Appalachia*, 25.
106 Ibid., 416.
107 Kingsolver drew on Dickens's Tommy Traddles in creating Tommy Waddles, constructing a character with empathy and resolve.
108 Ibid., 520.
109 Ibid.
110 Ibid.
111 Vance, 4.

Chapter 2

The Extractive Logic and the Climate Crisis in Gothic Appalachian Literature

Eighteenth-century explorers and settler colonials in Appalachia encountered massive old-growth forests and as early as 1742 discovered coal deposits alongside a river in West Virginia, marking the beginning of a highly covetous or vampiric approach to the region's natural resources that has shaped Appalachia ever since.[1] From deforestation to deep coal mining, and from mountaintop removal (MTR) to fracking, time and again an extractive logic has been applied to the region, a logic defined by profit margins and callous disregard for the health of the environment and local communities.

All too often when outsiders think of Appalachia, they struggle to see beyond stereotypes to acknowledge the costs of fossil fuel extraction. Instead, and by a cynical sleight of hand, rural Appalachia and its people are viewed as a foreboding threat, which neatly serves to deflect from the real horrors of extraction. Such misapprehensions are tightly woven into the popular imagination because it is more comforting to accept that rural Appalachians are gun-toting, toothless terrors, than it is to expose and recognize the real monster in the room. That monster, of course, is generated by extraction. In his work specifically on rural horror in Appalachia, McClanahan asks, "What if the horrifying reality of the rural is a result of the ways that those landscapes and people have been exploited and harmed by human activity and capital?"[2] For McClanahan, extraction wreaks havoc and devastation on both people and the environment, therefore across Appalachian literature extraction and the gothic are symbiotic, resulting in a body of work that writes back against fossil fuel extractivism, exposing its horrors and inequity.

Indeed, in her work on extraction and British literature, Elizabeth Carolyn Miller argues that "literary form and genre produce and extend extractivism as a mode of environmental understanding because of the deep and durational qualities of discourse." It is, she suggests, the "durational qualities of language, genre, and form" that ensures "literature engages with environmental materiality across time, and for this reason it is a crucial archive for understanding the relation between environmental history and environmental crises today."[3] As the region's authors depict the devastating impacts of an extractive logic, from deep coal mining to fracking, they add to a longer narrative arc about anthropogenic harm that intrinsically connects extraction and the climate crisis as we see in bell hooks's *Appalachian Elegy*, where all the "stripping removing destroying" in poem 48, can only lead to the "destiny of burning heat" in poem 25.[4]

The Monsters and Demons of an Extractive Logic

Matthew S. Henry applies the term "extractive fictions […] to describe literature and other cultural forms that render visible the socioecological impacts of extractive capitalism and problematize extraction as a cultural practice." For Henry, "Extractive fictions render visible the crumbling epistemological foundations that have historically undergirded the unchecked, often violent accumulationist tendencies of extractive capitalism."[5] Such fiction brings the gothic into the everyday and exposes the costs of fossil fuels both at the point of extraction and in their substantial contribution to global carbon emissions. Appalachian writers of extractive fiction explore in rich and gothic detail the frictions that result when an extractive logic is applied to people and place, as Affrilachia poet Crystal Good makes clear in "Boom Boom" where the absolute destruction caused by MTR is laid bare: "**BOOM! BOOM!/Forever gone.**"[6] The irreversible horror of blasting mountaintops leads Rebecca R. Scott to ask, "once a mountain disappears, how do we know it was ever really there?" arguing that in its absence "It becomes a ghost,"[7] and Appalachian literature is deeply haunted by the devasting impacts of MTR and the other waves of extraction that creates the "bereft" land that Susan Deer Cloud details in her poem "Mountaintops, Appalachia" (2019).[8] In a famous address at the Appalachian Studies Association conference in Huntington, West Virginia, in 2008, writer and environmental activist Silas House railed against MTR, calling on his fellow Appalachians to shake off their apathy and to stop allowing an extractive logic to turn them into "the living dead."[9]

Writers including Gurney Norman, Breece D'J Pancake, Ann Pancake, Denise Giardina, Tawni O'Dell, Crystal Good and Michael Croley, and poets including Joeseph Bathanti and Jesse Graves all dwell on the immense costs of extraction, but Ann Pancake, Giardina and Croley particularly turn to the monstrous sludge or slurry piles that, under the force of heavy rain can break out and envelope communities. In Giardina's *The Unquiet Earth* (1992) when Dillion discovers the dam holding back the sludge is giving way, form reflects content as the narrative fragments:

the dull boom when the lake touches the fiery slate and a gray cloud swells, rises far up the mountain, another explosion and another and the rising cloud sweeps away the picket shack and the tipple fence before it falls to earth a whirlpool licks across the bottom, rips out a large electrical transformer

flames shoot to the top of Trace Mountain   the sky crackles[10]

Giardina echoes the horrors of actual slurry spills including the Buffalo Creek Flood on February 26, 1972, in Logan County, West Virginia. As Henry notes, the Buffalo Creek Flood and the more recent "Martin County, Kentucky, coal slurry spill in 2000, which the EPA called the worst ever industrial disaster in the southeastern United States" mean the "likelihood of additional disaster looms," casting a dark shadow across Appalachian communities and throughout its literature.[11]

In "Washed Away" (2019), Croley, an author of dual Korean and Appalachian heritage, explores the experiences of Shin, a Korean man living in Kentucky with his husband Robert. Shin encounters the devastation wrought when a slurry pit above his in-law's home gives way and the "thick slurry, like wet, black concrete" pours down the mountainside.[12] The "sludge" comes "faster ripping through everything" and "the world turned black, the valley one big spilled bucket of paint that none of us could use but that would color our lives forever."[13] Time and again in Appalachian gothic literature characters witness the sheer horror of these unnatural landslides. Writing about the connection between flooding and MTR, journalist Francis X Clines notes, "With mountaintop removal, a fast, high-volume process that uses mammoth machinery to decapitate the coal rich hills that help define the hollows, the residents have become witnesses more than miners," and, in part, Appalachian extraction literature acts itself as witness.[14] While Croley's story ends on a more hopeful note as Shin imagines the new life that he, Robert, and his in-laws could begin somewhere beyond the Kentucky mountains, the devastation left by the slurry avalanche is a stark echo of the threats to so many communities across Appalachia, especially as weather patterns become more unstable.

Such looming threats hover over Pancake's *Strange As This Weather Has Been* (2007) where she rages against the environmental devastation of strip mining and MTR in West Virginia. Pancake utilizes minor character Avery to narrate the "history of slagheap disasters."[15] Avery, a survivor of the Buffalo Creek disaster, becomes obsessed with the history of coal operators in the region and he thinks his homeplace is "so subtly beautiful and so overlaid with doom. A haunt, a film coating all of it. Killed again and again, and each time, the place rising back on its haunches, diminished, but once more alive," yet he now worries deeply about the impacts of MTR, worrying that it will "finally beat the land for good."[16] Centuries of murdering the land have reduced it to a spectral "haunt," with layers of extraction superimposed, each new form becoming ever more monstrous and their threats made manifest in the massive slurry piles that threaten communities. However, both Pancake and Giardina's novels detail different forms of local activism against coal companies, pushing back against the stereotypes that present Appalachians as victims and/or passionate proponents of extraction.

The voracious pursuit of fossil fuels that resulted in the fracking boom in the early twenty-first century offers no exception to the gothic forms of extractive logic and several contemporary authors reflect on this particular form of extraction.[17] As an area rich in natural gas, the Marcellus Shale, which sits under the Appalachian basin, has been a prime target for fracking, so it is little surprise that Appalachian authors have turned to this most recent extractive horror. In Jennifer Haigh's *Heat and Light* (2016), set in Pennsylvania, comparisons are drawn between the "inhuman heart" of the oil boom that brought both boom and bust in an earlier time,[18] leaving ghost towns in its wake, with the rapid and voracious drive to frack.[19]

In the novel, the oil boom's earlier monstrosity is matched by fracking machines that make the land demonstrably "sicker" because "what lies beneath is altered forever."[20] In his work on hydrofracking fiction, Jason Molesky argues that "the toxicity of hydrofracking, along with the garish suppression of knowledge about it, situates most hydrofracking literature firmly within the realm of the gothic,"[21] suggesting that Haigh's novel "derives much of its force from the way that it repurposes conventions long associated with the gothic novel."[22] Gothic tropes certainly abound across Appalachian fracking literature, as we also see in Mesha Maren's debut novel *Sugar Run* (2018).[23] Primarily set in West Virginia, where central protagonist Jodi McCarty has returned after serving 18 years in prison, the bucolic, prelapsarian memories of her grandmother's farm give way to reality when she arrives home to discover expansive fracking operations across the locale.

In both novels, the fracking towers are monstrous. In his study of fracking, Tom Wilber notes that because "extracting the gas is difficult [...] it requires unconventional methods and infrastructure." This means "Shale gas pads tend to be four to six times larger than conventional single-acre pads" and the "bigger size is required for the greater number of tank farms, reservoirs, mixing areas, waste pits, pipes, equipment, and trucks needed to drill and stimulate a horizontal well."[24] In *Heat and Light*, the surface rig is vast, and when Rich stands at the bottom of the platform, the "noise is epic" and there is a "titanic whoosh of air."[25] Similarly, in *Sugar Run*, when Jodi first looks at the mountains where fracking towers continue to appear, she watches one old homeplace where "the white metal tower climbed into the cloudless sky and hoses spilled like loose intestines across the muddy ground," this uncanny monster bearing its innards in plain sight.[26] Jodie cannot help but feel that the fracking operations represent "real doom."[27] Fracking, with its obtrusive, extraneous and gigantic equipment, is doom-laden, its noises and fires ever-present: in *Sugar Run*, "The fire at the top of the tower throbbed, a perfect Pentecostal tongue of flame,"[28] what an attorney working on behalf of residents against fracking companies in *Heat and Light* simply terms, "a fracking nightmare."[29]

Haigh and Maren both utilize gothic tropes to depict the infrastructural brutalism of fracking and the experiences of people who daily encounter that violence. In his work on infrastructural brutalism and necropolitics, Michael Truscello asks that we "consider how infrastructure is always visible to and for some, and how art in particular can contribute to the subtle or dramatic shifts in public perceptions of infrastructure, especially in the context of late capitalism and global ecological collapse."[30] Haigh and Maren's novels contribute to understanding about how fracking operations and the neoliberal push to extract as much fossil fuel as possible before nations enforce net zero targets, continue to destroy both land and water at the point of extraction and contribute more widely to carbon emissions and the climate crisis.

As is common in both scientific reports and novels about fracking, *Heat and Light* and *Sugar Run* focus on its impact on waterways.[31] Writing about shale gas development (SGD), drinking water and infant health, Elaine L. Hill and Lala Ma point out that "SGD operations have the potential to cause groundwater contamination in all stages of the SGD life cycle,"[32] but that future work is still required to understand the full extent of SGD water contamination.[33] While scientists continue to research and deliberate, and fracking companies continue to downplay, deny and in some cases silence any direct correlations drawn between hydraulic fracturing and local waterways, authors work within the spaces between these positions.[34] In Haigh's novel, within a week of the fracking near Rich's home, his tap water becomes "cloudy" with a "rainbow film" on "the surface, like a spill of gasoline."[35] In *Sugar Run*, Maren employs Jodie's neighbor Farren to expose the impact of fracking on waterways when he shows her what fracking has done to his water:

> "Watch," he said, pulling a lighter from his pocket. He lit it and held it under the stream, and the water leapt, spurted, and then burst into flame. Jodi jumped back but Farren held steady as water poured down between his feet and the fire puffed up into his face [...]

Farren looked up, "Methane. Them gas companies have piped it up from the middle of the earth." He stared down again at the clear stream circled by a juddering ball of flame.[36]

The uncanniness of drinking water going up in flames takes on a more acute haunting because in both novels the link between fracking and changes to drinking water is something that is simultaneously known yet rendered unknown.

Despite the hypervisibility of fracking and various studies producing evidence of the harmful effects of hydraulic fracturing on waterways, fracking companies continue to obfuscate, a point Haigh highlights when Rich challenges a worker about the changes in his tap water. The worker tells him, "We're nowheres near your well we're drilling a mile down," providing him instead with a business card for the company's director of communications.[37] It is useful to think of attempts to conceal knowledge about the negative impacts of fracking in light of Avery Gordon's work on haunting. Gordon argues, "Hypervisibility," such as the hypervisibility of fracturing infrastructure, creates the sense that "not only that everything can be seen, but also that everything is available and accessible for our consumption," as in Haigh's novel where the hypervisibility of the fracking infrastructure lends itself to a narrative of openness and the conviction that there is nothing else to be seen.[38] In fracking literature the repressed cannot be contained and gothic tropes are deployed to chart a counternarrative of environmental destruction, both at the source of fracking operations and the various sites where fracking waste is illegally dumped.

Chris Offutt turns to the horrors of fracking waste in *Shifty's Boys*. During a murder investigation, a mysterious substance on the victim's boots leads Mick Hardin to the so-called mushroom mines, a disused limestone quarry with a complex history that has recently been purchased by a company to illegally dump fracking waste.[39] Offutt introduces Dr. Harker, an academic at Rocksalt State College, to depart knowledge about the waste, and she defines the fracking by-product as "Toxic as hell." She qualifies, "can't drink it or shower in it or use it in your garden. They have to dispose of it." Harker goes on to inform Mick that while "Kentucky's law forbids importing radioactive waste [...] there's a landfill down in Estill County with two thousand tons of it beside an elementary school."[40] Offutt draws here on the case of the Blue Ridge Landfill in Estill County, Kentucky, located near two schools where during the height of the fracking boom radioactive fracking waste was illegally dumped.[41] In the novel, Mick never discovers the source of this fracking waste, but wherever its origin, the waste shows contemptible, corporate disregard for local people, waterways, and biodiversity, and while

Mick puts an end to the illegal dumping of fracking waste, his conversation with Dr. Harker, and Offutt's echo of real-life instances of companies using Appalachia as a cesspool, indicate the illegal dumping of radioactive fracking waste is much more widespread and not as easily resolved as Mick's case. As Thorpe argues, "The relentless pursuit of profit leaves an apocalyptic trail of [...] environmental destruction" and a "swamp of toxic pollution" that cannot easily be remedied.[42]

Gothic Appalachian Literature and the Climate Crisis

If fossil fuel extraction is one side of the coin, then climate change sits firmly on the other, and in contemporary fiction, the climate crisis is no longer only projected onto horror-filled dystopian futures but also explored in realist texts that explore the impacts on lives, human and non-human, across the globe today, from wildfires and floods to the sixth mass extinction. In Appalachian contemporary literature, it is increasingly common to find references to the climate crisis, even in texts preoccupied with other pressing issues. In Offutt's Mick Hardin series, the violence of the illicit drug trade and the illegal dumping of fracking waste, all take place against a backdrop of a changing world. In *Shifty's Boys* Mick's sister, Linda, out campaigning, sweats "through her uniform" and "discards the official hat," thinking "It was too early to be this hot—too early in spring and too early in the day—and the politicians were fighting over climate change," highlighting the failure of politics to fully grapple with the increasing impacts of the climate crisis.[43] Or, in Joy's noir novels where changing weather patterns are impossible to ignore: in *The Line That Held Us* "Seasons were strange [...] the world turning more peculiar as time passed. Nowadays, there might come two feet of snow that melted off by the next afternoon, then the day after that they were back to T-shirt weather in the middle of December."[44] Peculiar indeed, but a peculiar, or an uncanny, that is increasingly the new normal.

Such references to unnatural weather patterns bring the gothic out of the shadows because in the Anthropocene, as Hannah Stark, Katrina Schlunke, and Penny Edmonds argue, "The Anthropocene has rendered the familiar strange and the strange familiar."[45] That strangeness is captured in Jesse Graves's poem "Drought Year" (2014) where we witness the signs "of a permanently changing ecology."[46] In a region already shaped by an extractive logic and its attendant horrors, the battered landscape brings the risk of more acute climate threats. Writing about the severe flooding in Kentucky in July 2022 that killed 44 people and where "13 counties were declared federal disaster areas,"[47] Chelsea Harvey notes that "The enduring impact of mountaintop mining in Appalachia adds another layer of complexity" in an ironic turn where an "industry that heavily contributed to the acceleration of climate change may have also altered Appalachia's flood risks."[48] MTR and deforestation leave parts of Appalachia highly vulnerable and alongside flood risks, parts of the region have also witnessed devastating wildfires.

Indeed, several Appalachian authors have turned to the 2016 wildfires that raged across parts of the region, partly as a result of drought conditions. Across the world, wildfires are increasing in their intensity and duration and the fires in the fall of 2016 in Appalachia were no exception. As M. J. Reilly et al., outline, "ignitions across the region strained fire suppression efforts and ultimately resulted in more than thirty large fires burning simultaneously. The fires of fall 2016 were larger and burned more area than in the previous three decades combined."[49] Wildfires are the primary focus in Ed Roberson's poem "The Listening," from his recent collection *Asked What Has Changed* (2021). Pittsburgh-born Roberson reflects on the climate crisis from his home in Chicago, and in "The Listening," wonders whether we will, given the speed of wildfires, be "fast enough/to outdistance events."[50] The gothic Anthropocene looms large in this foreboding rhetorical question, and Justin Edwards, Rune Graulund and Johan Höglund, remind us that,

> To live in the Anthropocene is to recognize that transgression, excess, and monstrosity are no longer anomalies in human life but inextricable parts of it. Gothic has the power to unsettle readers more than most other literary or cultural forms because it dwells on widespread anxieties, dread, the horrific, the repellant, and achieves a *frisson* that other mimetic modes of representation can barely remember.[51]

Gothic frisson reverberates across the fiction of David Joy, Charles Dodd White, and Leah Hampton, who each explore the 2016 Appalachian wildfires.

In Joy's *When These Mountains Burn*, the link between extraction, the degradation of land, and the destruction of people are all deeply connected. The drought has left the "whole region […] dry as grain" and once the wildfires start, "soon as one fire burned out, windswept embers lit the next, scorching swaths of land left black in the wake."[52] Joy employs Raymond (Ray) Mathis, a one-time forester and now retired father trying and failing in the early part of the novel to save his drug-addicted son, to offer the most lucid ruminations on the fires. While Ray lays part of the blame of wildfires on forest mismanagement over several years, he also recognizes the changing climate, thinking about how winters have been warmer and snow "didn't fall like it used to."[53] The news is filled with details of fires spreading in neighboring Tennessee: we learn of an "entire community engulfed," and the gothic horrors of these devastating fires are made manifest by their spread into Gatlinburg and Pigeon Forge. Ray holds beloved memories of drives over the border into Tennessee with his wife and son, visiting these popular tourist destinations before his son's descent into addiction and his wife's terminal cancer. The uncanniness of entertainment sites ravaged by wildfires, including the image of "Cupid's Chapel of Love burning to the ground, its heart-shaped sign still standing while the building crippled to cinder and ash" shows how the climate crisis, the monster of our own making, wreaks havoc on all things.[54]

Where Joy juxtaposes the wildfires with drug addiction, fellow contemporary Appalachian authors, Charles Dodd White and Leah Hampton contrast them with political, far-right extremism in the wake of Donald Trump's election victory in 2016, forming part of what I am terming here a post-Trump moment in Appalachian literature. For Elizabeth Catte, author of *What You Are Getting Wrong About Appalachia* (2018), the region "has become symbolic of the forces that gave us Donald Trump [...] And the region's conservative voters, who have been profiled endlessly, have been a reliable stand-in for all Trump voters, absorbing the outrage of progressive readers." For Catte, such readings depend on "tired oversimplifications" and arise out of "a failure of imagination."[55] Responding to that failure of imagination, White and Hampton utilize the gothic nature of the 2016 wildfires to write back against the blind alignment of the region with Trump, and, as Andrew Smith and William Hughes remind us, "The Gothic seems to be the form which [...] provides a culturally significant point of contact between literary criticism, ecocritical theory and political process."[56]

White's *How Fire Runs* (2020), starts in an intensely hot spring with little to no rainfall.[57] Published in 2020, White was writing the novel in the wake of the 2016 drought conditions and wildfires across Tennessee, and in a time when global wildfires have increased in both intensity and duration. Indeed, the summer of 2019, a year before the novel was published was, according to Daniel Mathews, "one of the worst on record for fires—globally."[58] As a result, the title *How Fire Runs*, simultaneously refers to both far-right ideology and climate change, and White applies gothic tropes as he represents the two crises and the differing approaches to them.

In the novel readers might expect the demon to be Gavin Noon, the far-right, neo-Nazi extremist who plans to establish his very own "Little Europe" community in Elizabethton, Tennessee, emboldened by Trump's rhetoric and support of far-right groups. White specifically pinpoints the exact cause of Noon's rise with a local environmental activist in the novel underlining the need to be "part of the resistance. We all do what we can do with the pussy-grabber-in-chief holding office."[59] Noon is presented as deeply monstrous, a strange creature made possible by the populism spouted from the White House during Trump's presidency. He is "a creature of mere shape and motion"[60] who believes there "was nothing wrong in agreeing with the nighttime in his soul," and who prowls around in the dark, stalking his political prey.[61] Yet while the threat of the far-right is real and appeared to be spreading rapidly across Western democracies in the period White was writing the novel, epitomized by the result of the 2016 Brexit referendum in the United Kingdom and the rise of populist leaders such as Donald Trump, the novel exposes the even greater risk of missing or denying the signs of climate change that threaten more than political systems.[62]

So preoccupied by defeating Noon, White's central protagonist, Democrat Kyle Pettus, pays such little attention to the drought conditions that he is thoroughly bewildered by the wildfire at the novel's close. Kyle is unable to fully see the portent in the drought, its seriousness overshadowed in his mind by Noon and the threat he poses to the community. Yet readers may be underwhelmed by Noon's defeat: as a gothic monster, he is perhaps too easily vanquished. Politically defeated and unable to reconcile his losses, Noon takes his own life before the novel ends: with one gothic villain undone, White's central protagonists now face an even greater threat in the form of the wildfire sweeping across the community, a fire intensified by the incredibly dry spell preceding it.

A storm hits the county on the night of the election and its winds fuel the wildfires. The wind tears and howls across the landscape and when it reaches a human-started fire, it flings the flames "across the river and up the shoulders and sides of the mountains in a matter of minutes." The "firestorm detonated abruptly as a bomb and the earth ruptured."[63] In the inverted world at the end of the novel, the burning ridgelines send ash down on to the streets where it lies "like an awful dry snow"[64] and "the scene [...] was battle strewn. Exploded and flame-guttered trees."[65] The explosions and "battle strewn" landscape are a new and horrific turn that Kyle can no longer entirely ignore. White's novel warns not only about the threat populism poses to democracy but also the existential risks posed by the climate crisis: readers are left wondering if whether the same airtime was devoted to the climate as it is to populist figures such as Donald Trump, more might be done to achieve net zero goals and mitigate against the worst impacts of human-made climate change. The horrific wildfire in the novel, representative of the increasingly intensified and widespread wildfires across the globe in recent years, are some of the impacts felt as the planet reached 1°C of warming above pre-industrial levels in approximately 2017.[66] With climate change impacts already so devastating at this degree of warming, White's novel portends a bleak future where once dystopian landscapes become the new normal unless action is taken.

Emerging Appalachian author Leah Hampton also turns to the 2016 wildfires and politics in her short story "Boomer" (2020) where Larry, a forest service ranger, whose marriage falls apart around him throughout the story, worries about the wildfires that might spread after "a long drought, five states wide." In preparation for what might unfold in a tinderbox landscape, his work crew is "spooked." The impending sense of doom is intensified by the 2016 election that dominates the news and "firehouse chatter."[67] As the anticipated wildfires do their worst, the forest is rendered "cinematic at night, with lit slithers of amber inching in chiaroscuro through the trees and blackness."[68] The slithering flames and the traces of amber in the night sky are a disturbing warning made manifest in the "Blazzing tendrils of ladder fire, a full-on front burning from root to kudzu to canopy" that feed "themselves" on the wind. Larry watches "the updrafts gorging themselves on air [...] the scene burned bright and hellish."[69] Larry is overwhelmed by this burning world, and with no respite from the fires at the end of the story, Hampton pulls the fires and politics together in Larry's rueful assessment: "Another blaze rising out of Transylvania would soon join theirs, doubling the conflagration. In Tennessee people were dying, suffocating in their cars as they tried to escape. That, at least, had made the papers, alongside all the stories blaming mountain people for picking the president. Larry didn't know anyone who'd had the time to vote."[70] From White's democratic characters to Hampton's firefighters too exhausted battling the flames to vote, we see Appalachian writers pushing back against the idea of a monolithic "Trump country."

While states including West Virginia and Tennessee voted overwhelmingly for Trump, those statistics only tell part of the story and add to further reductive understandings of the region. If White and Hampton focus on the risk of ignoring the climate crisis as populist figures suck up all the oxygen, then Frank X Walker and Nikky Finney offer searing attacks against Trump and his policies. In Walker's collection *Masked Man, Black: Pandemic and Protest Poems* (2020) among the many critiques he makes across these poems about the 45th president, he points particularly in "2020 Vision" to the problems caused by a leader and administration that "deny science and climate change."[71] Similarly, in "The Good Fight, Again," collected in *Love Child's Hotbed of Occasional Poetry* (2020), Finney charts the multitudinous threats posed by Trump, including his bidding for those who do not "believe in one more environmental protection/order, one more solar windmill turning on the/plains."[72] Walker and Finney offer salient reminders of the threats Trump poses not only to the U.S. political system but also to global efforts to tackle the climate crisis.

Climate change emerges in many ways across the region's literature and in moves that go beyond the limits of anthropogenic thinking, non-human ghosts are frequent occurrences. Species extinction results in different forms of haunting, both in the ghostly presence of animals believed to be extinct or the shadowy sightings of the endangered. More widely, in *A Dream in Which*

I Am Playing With Bees (2024) R. K. Fauth, a New York-born poet who now lives in Appalachia, imagines a future where bees are extinct and explores life in this post-bee future. The poems are not just about biodiversity loss, but, as Fauth writes in her introduction, the question of "what happens to our creative faculties, or language in general, after a peg in the environment is removed?"[73] Fauth's poems expose the deep connections between the natural world and human language, and while human life continues after the bees are gone, species loss is profoundly haunting. As Edwards, Graulund, and Höglund indicate, "there is something inherently uncanny, dark, and haunting about an era defined by a 'dark ecology' of rising temperatures and seas, microplastics and extreme weather, the decline of the Arctic [...] and the sixth mass extinction." In this period of climate crisis, they argue "we are left in the paradoxical position of having a greater impact on nature than ever before, while at the same time experiencing a profound sense of loss and agency when it comes to its continued existence."[74] That paradox is at the center of Matthew Neill Null's short story, "Natural Resources," about the black bear population in West Virginia and its cycles of near extinction, reintroduction, and extinction as humans battle with their own anthropogenic desire to tame nature while longing for the animals when their numbers dwindle.[75]

In the story the reintroduced bears readily adapt to the "stony land" and "other ruined places," finding homes in abandoned strip mines and quarries, but when the reintroduction becomes too successful a "new management plan" is drawn up in distant offices "under flickering florescent lights."[76] The omniscient narrator's contempt is laid bare for the administrators and managers drawing up action plans under artificial light, thoroughly divorced from the reality on the ground. Null draws on West Virginia's attempts to manage its black bear population and in the story, human–bear encounters prove so frightening that new and horrific hunting measures are introduced that lead to waves of hunters and men "with arms dipped in blood" ready to illegally sell bear gallbladders to Chinese buyers.[77] When the "Bear Hunters Association" wins public support for an "open season in spring and summer," a route to extinction begins. Chased around, "the bears couldn't store enough fat for hibernation," resulting in higher winter morbidity rates and the horrific knowledge that cubs are "aborted in the womb" and "Old sows crawled back in caves and never came out. The population dropped 65 percent." A final push is made to save the bears, but it takes just "a few malingering years" to mark "the end of bears in Tuscarora," the bears so desperate in the end "they seemed to fling themselves in front of the guns," rendered suicidal by human bloodlust.[78] With the bears gone, humans and insurance companies, armed with "algorithms" turn on the deer population: "there are so many deer, so many wrecks."[79] In this deeply satirical story Null exposes a human-first approach, one that fails to develop sustainable ways to live with nature and propels the sixth mass extinction.

Species extinction intersects with environmental degradation and eco-terrorism in Mark Powell's *Lioness* (2022), another key novel forming part of the post-Trump moment in Appalachian literature.[80] Playwright David Wood is working through the aftermath of the deaths of his son, Daniel, and wife, Mara. Their son dies of non-Hodgkin's lymphoma, which his wife attributes to him drinking the contaminated water David brought home for investigative research. In her despair, and what she learns about the toxicity of the water ("Aldrin, dieldrin, DDT") and its connection to "RAIN!" a water-bottling plant in southwest Virginia, the activism that shaped the early part of Mara and David's life together is reawakened.[81]

Early in their relationship they lived in a community founded by eco-activist and terrorist Chris Bright, and detailed insights into Chris' life open a plethora of polluting industries, including the coal power plant, Erwin Power, where his uncle worked. At 51, his uncle dies, emaciated and looking "seventy," like "a scarecrow," a death Chris directly attributes to the power company.[82] We later learn that while Erwin Power denies "the presence of heavy metals in the drinking water of a community," the EPA "measured contamination at a thousand times the legal limit," but by the time its findings are released, "a baby was already dead and several women were having hysterectomies."[83] Chris's frustrations with the inequity of a system where the most significant criminals never face justice is encapsulated in the 45th president. He thinks:

> All the shit of the twenty-first century and who had gone to jail? Who had paid? [...] Name someone locked up from Blackwater or the Pentagon or the Heritage Foundation. How about Purdue Pharma? The answer was none of them, not a goddamn one. Donald J. Trump was in office for god's sake.
> And who had paid?[84]

Chris's questions about a lack of accountability highlight a marked shift in the first decades of twenty-first century where there has been exponential rise in levels of impunity. David Crane, drawing on Leila Sadat's accountability paradigm, argues that "holding accountable those who commit" atrocities is "a challenging proposition today" in a world of "Fake news, untruths, conspiracy theory, all mixed by the misunderstood impact of social media."[85] Crane draws on *Alice in Wonderland* to describe the turned-upside-down nature of this contemporary moment, a nightmare-filled world where even the most obvious high crimes go unpunished. Chris is particularly attune to the inequities and horrors of this new age of impunity, deciding it is his responsibility to bring about justice at any price. After Daniel's death, Mara finds her way back to Chris and the two plan and execute a bombing at the RAIN! Facility. Powell never sidelines the complexities around eco-terrorism, using Mara, Chris and David to explore questions about climate activism, and as he does so, he shows the different guises of terrorism: while Mara and Chris undertake acts of domestic ecoterrorism, the novel also exposes the sinister, quieter, but no less impactful terrorism inflicted upon communities for financial and political power.

Powell depicts an Appalachia under attack, a region that David considers, "has consistently been drained of resources, polluted, shit on."[86] All these terrors are on David's mind, and it is no coincidence that his first successful production, *High Water*, is "an eco-play," an "environmental jeremiad," in which the world cannot be saved: "the planet is terminal."[87] David reflects on Mara's bouts of sadness even before Daniel's death, wondering if what she felt was "simply life in the Anthropocene, in the Sixth Extinction? The self-care while the dioxins flow into the groundwater. The meditation apps while the atmosphere ignites and the elephants die and we are all delivered to the grave via Amazon Prime."[88] Powell taps into the hidden horrors of the present moment as life marches on with consumers distracted and politicians struggling to find consensus on addressing the climate crisis both within and beyond national borders. It is easier, of course, to ignore the climate crisis and the sixth mass extinction, but Powell demands, via complex questions about climate action and environmental terrorism, that readers contemplate their own lives in the Anthropocene.

The latest mass extinction is largely played out in the novel through the characters' obsession with mountain lions and panthers, large cats commonly referenced in Appalachian literature, their ghostly presences and mysterious sightings a haunting reminder of humankind's impact on the natural world.[89] Chris, Mara, and David are each obsessed with a lioness, a stuffed and mounted lioness that connects all three. When Chris and later Mara first see the stuffed animal, they are mesmerized. For Mara, "It looked like something from either the ancient past or the distant future, a relic, or a thing not yet realized."[90] It is deeply haunting, a ghostly symbol of the already gone and a harbinger of all that might be lost in the sixth mass extinction. Constantly reminded that mountain lions no longer exist in Appalachia, that they are now the stuff of supposed sightings and the stories of old-timers, David is haunted by the ideas of lions, convinced that a lion prowls around and inside his house. The stories of lions and the stuffed lioness are a spectral force throughout the novel, somehow both there and not there, not extinct and extinct, much in the way David imagines Mara and Daniel.

In vignettes that open and close the novel, David gives Mara and Daniel a different life. In his mind, Mara and Daniel live in Florida, surrounded by the nature they both loved, and even though their ideal world is not untouched by the climate crisis Mara finds peace and contentment with the knowledge that "Things will change, things will disappear."[91] A figment of David's imagination, this Mara achieves the peace she could not find in life. In his mind, she is devoid of anger, their son still lives, and there is no desire to enact revenge via ecoterrorism. Here David is guilty of not being able to truly face reality without Mara and Daniel. His reality is a world radically altered by the climate crisis, a world where everyone is experiencing a "different future, the one we knew was coming but has surprised us just the same […] The waters rose—just as they said they would. The air is hotter and dirtier, the infections longer and deadlier […] each day a little warmer, a little grimmer, a little harder to breathe."[92] It is therefore preferable to imagine Mara and Daniel who, despite also being witnesses to the climate crisis, take joy in small moments. Powell leaves David wondering, "What if that is enough?", the question looms large at the end of the novel, with readers left to ponder what is at stake in any answer.

The gothic is a vital resource as authors explore the devastating logic of extraction that harms people and place, profoundly impacting the biosphere at the point of extraction, the climate crisis, and the sixth mass extinction. Edwards, Graulund, and Höglund explore the "narrative strategies for the Anthropocene," arguing such strategies "are necessarily speculative, and often dark, in nature."[93] As Appalachian literature about extraction and the climate crisis attests, gothic tropes aptly capture the monstrosity of extractive infrastructure and the horrors of wildfires. This is particularly profound in contemporary literature where the climate crisis is not a far-off threat, and where the connections between fossil fuel extraction and the climate crisis are no longer the projections of scientists or information that can be easily denied by fossil fuel companies. Edwards, Graulund, and Höglund highlight the concern that "by foregrounding the 'anthropos' of current 'cene' (era), we are in danger of erasing and smoothing out not just important links between cause and effect but also responsibility and culpability."[94] Contemporary Appalachian gothic literature is one place where the causes and effects of the climate crisis are difficult to ignore. In a discussion of Pancake's *Strange as This Weather Has Been*, Nathaniel Otjen argues that "As a site of energy extraction, material accumulation, and landscape erasure, the Appalachian coalfields are, in many ways, at the center of Anthropocene concerns and narratives in the United States."[95] In spaces such as Appalachia, where fossil fuel extraction and the climate crisis intersect, the true horrors of humankind's anthropogenic approach are laid bare in all their visceral monstrosity.

Notes

1 For a history and personal reflection on living in an extraction zone, see: Giardina, "Appalachian Images."
2 McClanahan, "Earth-world-planet," 641.
3 Miller, *Extraction Ecologies and the Literature of the Long Exhaustion*, 3.
4 hooks, bell, *Appalachian Elegy: Poetry and Place*, 58 and 35. Copyright © 2012 Gloria Jean Watkins (bell hooks). Reprinted by permission of The University Press of Kentucky.
5 Henry, "Extractive Fictions and Postextraction Futurisms," 407.
6 Good, *Valley Girl*, 22.
7 Scott, *Removing Mountains*, 1.
8 Deer Cloud, "Mountaintops, Appalachia," 104.
9 House, "A Conscious Heart," 10.
10 Giardina, *The Unquiet Earth*, 329.
11 Henry, *Hydronarratives*, 86.
12 Croley, *Any Other Place: Stories*, 199.
13 Ibid., 202–203.
14 Clines, "Flooding in Appalachia Stirs Outrage Over a Mining Method."
15 Ibid., 236.
16 Ibid., 239.
17 For an interesting overview of several key novels that explore fracking, see Nash, "Fracking Novels: Scrabble, Zombies, and the Problematized Real," 60–63.
18 Haigh, *Heat and Light*, 4.
19 For accounts of the boom then bust cycle of fracking, see Jerolmack, "The Fracking Boom is Over. Where did All the Jobs Go?"
20 Haigh, 358–359.
21 Molesky, "Gothic Toxicity and the Mysteries of Nondisclosure in American Hydrofracking Literature," 53.
22 Ibid., 67.
23 Maren, *Sugar Run*.
24 Wilber, *Under the Surface*, 59–60.
25 Haigh, 259.
26 Maren, 249.
27 Ibid., 244.
28 Ibid., 234.
29 Haigh, 319.
30 Truscello, 26.
31 See the EPA's "Hydraulic Fracturing for Oil and Gas: Impacts from the Hydraulic Fracturing Water Cycle on Drinking Water Resources in the United States (Final Report)."
32 Hill and Ma, "Drinking Water, Fracking, and Infant Health," 3.
33 Ibid., 16.
34 While the fracking debate is fraught, with claims and counterclaims put forth persistently by those in favor and those against fracking, fracking companies actively silenced claims about damages to water supplies. For a report on how fracking companies employed non-disclosure agreements to silence knowledge about the damage to waterways, see Efstathiou Jr. and Drajem, "Fracking Companies Silence Water Complaints with Sealed Settlements."

35　Haigh, 258.
36　Maren, 197.
37　Haigh, 259.
38　Gordon, *Ghostly Matters*, 16.
39　Offutt, *Shifty's Boys*, 124–126.
40　Ibid., 174–175.
41　For details about the illegal dumping of fracking waste in Estill County, Kentucky, see Gaffney's "A Small Town's Battle Against Radioactive Fracking Waste," and *Appalachian Citizens' Law Center's* "Estill County Radioactive Fracking Waste."
42　Thorpe, 6.
43　Offutt, *Shifty's Boys*, 85.
44　Joy, *The Line That Held Us*, 146–147.
45　Stark, Schlunke, and Edmonds, "Introduction," 22.
46　Graves, *Basin Ghosts*, 50–52.
47　See: Klesta, "Resilience and Recovery."
48　See: Harvey, "We are Climate Zero."
49　Reilly, et al., "Drivers and Ecological Impacts of a Wildfire Outbreak in the Southern Appalachian Mountains after Decades of Fire Exclusion," 3.
50　Roberson, "The Listening" in *Asked What Has Changed*, 31.
51　Edwards, Graulund, and Höglund, "Introduction," xi–xii.
52　Joy, *When These Mountains Burn*, 6.
53　Ibid., 94.
54　Ibid., 253.
55　Catte, "Why 'Trump Country isn't as Republican as you Think'."
56　Smith and Hughes, "Introduction," 5.
57　White, *How Fire Runs*.
58　Mathews, *Trees in Trouble*, 237.
59　White, 121.
60　Ibid., 69.
61　Ibid., 41.
62　Since White wrote *How Fire Runs*, there have been several far-right election victories in Europe including in Italy in 2022 and the Netherlands in 2023.
63　White, 241.
64　Ibid., 252.
65　Ibid., 255.
66　See the IPPC's "Global Warming of 1.5°C: Special Report: FAQ Chapter 1," particularly the response to frequently asked question 1.2 "How close are we to 1.5°C?" for an overview of when the planet reached 1°C.
67　Hampton, *Fuckface and Other Stories*, 15.
68　Ibid., 21.
69　Ibid., 23.
70　Ibid., 26.
71　Walker, *Masked Man, Black: Pandemic and Protest Poems*, 70.
72　Finney, *Love Child's Hotbed of Occasional Poetry*, 165.
73　Fauth, *A Dream In Which I Am Playing With Bees*, 3.
74　Edwards, Graulund, and Höglund, xiv.
75　Null, *Allegheny Front*.
76　Ibid., 49.

77 See: Owen, "Living with Black Bears in West Virginia."
78 Null, 51.
79 Ibid., 52.
80 Powell, *Lioness*.
81 Ibid., 225.
82 Ibid., 150.
83 Ibid., 158.
84 Ibid., 287.
85 Crane, "Alice in Wonderland: Atrocity and Accountability in the 21st Century, A World Turned Upside Down," 35.
86 Ibid., 53.
87 Ibid., 32.
88 Ibid. 259.
89 See: Goff, "Cougar: Ghost of Appalachia."
90 Powell, 77.
91 Ibid., 314.
92 Ibid., 313.
93 Edwards, Graulund, and Höglund, xv.
94 Ibid., xxii.
95 Otjen, "When Things Hail," 296.

Chapter 3

Race and LGBTQ+ Rights in Gothic Appalachian Literature

Teresa Goddu saliently notes that "the American gothic is haunted by race" and that "when race is restored to the *darkness* of American literature, the gothic reappears as a viable category."[1] Goddu also traces the emergence of the southern gothic, where slavery, segregation, and systemic racism heavily influence the region's gothicism. By necessity, as a subgenre within both the American and southern gothic, the Appalachian gothic is haunted by slavery and settler colonization. Engaging with this haunting past and its impacts on the present is a critical part of challenging the misconceptions of the region. Writing from both rural and urban experiences, Indigenous, Black, immigrant, and first-generation writers play a critical role in challenging and rewriting the region, often exploring intersectionality at the crossroads of race, class, gender, and sexuality, and this chapter moves from a discussion of race to LGBTQ+ rights. As Hilary Glasby, Sherrie Gradin, and Rachael Ryseron argue, "Appalachian queerness remains underrepresented, misunderstood, sometimes muted, and sometimes invisible."[2] The Appalachian gothic plays a significant role in exposing historical and contemporaneous injustices and prejudices across the region and challenges the failure to register Appalachia's complexity and diversity.

Engaging with the region's diversity obviously serves to write back against monolithic ideas of Appalachian culture as white, heteronormative, masculine, and conservative, ideas that were reinforced after the 2016 presidential election, and the stamp of "Trump Country" that marked out Appalachia, aligning it with the "racism, cruelty, bigotry and abuse" that were the hallmarks of Donald Trump's campaign and presidency.[3] In a period where hard-won equal rights for women and LGBTQ+ people are threatened, and far-right populism across Western democracies stirs up what McCollum lists as "the stench of slavery, anti-Semitism, genocide, fascism, and neo-Nazism," as well as Islamophobia, it is vital to explore the ways Appalachian authors, both before and since 2016, have deployed the gothic to expose how such sentiments were never fully expunged and what is at stake in their frightful resurgence.[4]

Race and Gothic Appalachian Literature

Appalachia's racial diversity has a long and complicated history. Essays across William H. Turner and Edward J. Cabbell's edited collection *Blacks in Appalachia*, "demonstrate that Black Appalachians were some of America's *first* blacks—appearing almost a century before the landing at Jamestown."[5] Those first Black Appalachians, Theda Perdue outlines, "lived within the domain of the Cherokee Indians," and southern Appalachia was home to several Indigenous nations and peoples prior to colonization in the sixteenth century.[6] H. Tyler Blethen reminds us that while the "Cherokee dominated southern Appalachia," the "Creeks, Choctaws, Chickasaws, and Shawnees" also populated the region before being forcefully removed with the Cherokees in the 1830s.[7] For Eric Gary Anderson and Melanie Benson Taylor, "Indigenous literatures of the South have always been both future-minded and profoundly haunted."[8] As they indicate, as well as being future focused, southern Indigenous writing, which includes Appalachian Indigenous literature, is also deeply haunted by forced removal and genocide. To differing extents, two contemporary novels about the Eastern Band of Cherokee Indians (EBCI) that are both "future-minded" and expose the hauntings and horrors of settler colonialism, importantly disrupt the stereotypical associations of Appalachia with whiteness: Blake M. Hausman's[9] *Riding the Trail of Tears* (2011)[10] and Annette Saunooke Clapsaddle's *Even As We Breathe* (2020), dissect historic and present-day injustices as they write Indigenous people back into the narratives that have excluded them.[11]

Hausman's *Riding the Trail of Tears* is a futuristic satire set at a theme park in north Georgia: "TREPP—Tsalagi Removal Exodus Point Park."[12] The major attraction at TREPP is a "digital universe" where visitors experience the Trail of Tears, a virtual world designed by Arthur (Art) Wilson, grandfather of Tallulah Wilson, whose post-college career is bound up in her grandfather's legacy.[13] Tallulah is a tour guide on the ride, and unbeknownst to Art, Tallulah, or the visitors, this digital world does not operate entirely of its own accord. Inside the system exist "the real Nunnehi" or Little Little people, and the novel is narrated by one of the Little Little People who has escaped the system and entered Tallulah's mind. Hausman deploys the Little Little People to represent loss of culture and orality, with the Little Little People having been expunged from Cherokee storytelling in a period of revolution predating European colonialization. The narrator reminds readers that "when you get cut from the spoken word, it's hard to come back."[14]

The haunting nature of the ride is immediately apparent to the young Tallulah when her grandfather first allows her to step into his retrofitted Jeep Cherokee that provides a virtual route into the past and the bloody, violent removal of Indigenous peoples. We learn "Arthur and Tallulah rode the whole Trail of Tears that night, all the way from the stockades in Georgia to the hills and lakes in northeastern Oklahoma [...] A mass of bent and broken bodies that stretched up to ten miles long at the beginning of the trip [...] Tallulah's feet felt bruised and raw."[15] For Art, only by experiencing the "whole Trail of Tears" will future visitors gain a better understanding of the horrors and terrors of removal. Yet we learn that many guests deliberately find ways to kill their virtual identities before the end of the Trail because they want to see Medicine Man, the stereotypical "Indian" loved by tourists who, despite what they have seen on the Trail, continue to struggle to understand and engage with actual history.

At the start of the novel Tallulah takes tour group 5709 into the ride that they access via "the Chamber," an aptly named entry point into a space where violent history is played out on an endless loop.[16] Yet, with one Little Little Person having escaped the system, this day is like no other: the Little Little People stage their own revolt and one member of 5709, elderly Irma Rosenberg, is separated from the group. As the two storylines play out inside the trail, both Tallulah and Irma wrestle with what Irma comes to recognize as "a digital death house."[17] In usually concealed spaces, Irma meets the "Misfits," hidden characters being hunted by "the Suits," a group Gabriella Friedman interprets "as embodiments of the mechanisms that settler societies use to track, contain, and brutalize native people, including the legal system."[18] Certainly, when Tallulah enters the Misfit space toward the end of the novel, she is startled by the Misfits' clothing, garments that "represent several eras and changes in Cherokee fashion" including "Buckskins next to ribbon-shirts" and "Football jerseys and colorful cotton suits." This, Tallulah thinks, is not "supposed to happen," she has "never witnessed nonstandard non-1830s standard clothing inside the Trail of Tears."[19] Bearing witness, Tallulah is faced with the recognition that her grandfather's virtual experience is not limited to the horrors of removal but has also absorbed the injustices inflicted upon the Cherokee ever since.

To that end, there is a ghost in the system, but the ghost is manifold, representing layer upon layer of crimes and discrimination. As Thomas Rain Crowe writes in his poem "Narrenturm," "Terror/results from even the smallest history of pain" and in the novel the virtual ride has absorbed Indigenous pain from the most obvious acts of brutality and genocide, to the less seen, but highly palpable degrees of pain suffered by Indigenous communities across time.[20] Irma, the witness to the additional layers of haunting beyond the Trail of the Tears, comes to feel guilt and shame for having wanted to ride the Trail so poorly educated about the EBCI, both in terms of historic and present day injustices.

More recently, Annette Saunooke Clapsaddle explores the haunting legacy of settler colonialism for the EBCI in *Even As We Breathe*, a novel set in North Carolina against the backdrop of World War II. Her narrator, Cowney Sequoyah, a 19-year-old ruled out of the war due to a birth defect, leaves the reservation to work for the summer at the Grove Park Inn and Resort in Asheville, a place transformed from a hotel into a holding facility for Axis diplomats. Death, bones, and haunting run though the novel, and Erica Abrams Locklear argues that "By centering EBCI as the main characters supported by a cast of minor white characters, Clapsaddle re-envisions the false idea of a monolithically white Appalachia at the same time she invites readers to broaden perceptions of Appalachian literature."[21] As the first novel published by an enrolled member of the EBCI, *Even As We Breathe* is certainly an important contribution to challenging the common failure to acknowledge the region's diversity. Yet while Locklear is correct that the white characters are minor, their impact on the lives of the EBCI characters is unequivocal, from their casual and systemic racism to the missing child of one of the diplomats.

After discovering a bone on hotel land, a place reportedly "'built on graves,'" Cowney becomes the prime suspect when the girl disappears, and it is the interjection of white FBI agent, Jonathan Craig, who served with Cowney's father in World War I, that prevents Cowney from becoming another victim of injustice.[22] Saunooke Clapsaddle uses the disproportionate impact of the minor white characters in the novel to show how, even in a novel with an EBCI first-person narrator, white people cast a long shadow over the lives of Indigenous people. For Michelle Burnham, "it is the settler colonist whose face has taken up an unwelcome tenancy in the Native American home, and whose threatening presence haunts American Indian narrative."[23] By the end of the narrative, Cowney recognizes that the government buried the inconvenient truth about the death of the prisoner of war's child and that his account of that time disinters the story: "They tried to erase her […] her story was buried – was buried until now. I don't talk much of ceremony, a term so misunderstood and strip-mined, but that is all I know to call this. I offer her this rite."[24] Cowney, speaking from the present day, employs extractive language to draw together the destruction of both the land and aspects of EBCI culture. Yet, his final message is how the Appalachian Mountains "have ingested our bones for centuries so that we might renew this soil with memory […] We are the DNA strands criss-crossing these hills," in short, we are EBCI and Appalachian.[25] For Locklear, Saunooke Clapsaddle's intersectional approach "extends an open invitation to Appalachian storytellers of many disparate voices" and Cowney's journey writes back against the idea that a haunting past must be singularly debilitating.[26]

In her poetry collection, *madness like morning glories* (2005), doris davenport, also known as doris diosa davenport, similarly takes an intersectional approach as she explores the complex lives of the Black residents of Soque Street, Georgia, a street with a Cherokee name.[27] As a Black, self-identified "performance poet-writer-educator; a lesbian-feminist bi-amorous anarchist; working-class iconoclast from northeast Georgia," intersectionality is vital for Davenport as she explores the richness, vibrancy, and complexity of the community she depicts in her poetry sequence where she explores Indigenous and Black lives in Appalachia.[28] As Wester observes, through the gothic's "haunting specters [...] African American writers suggest that racial injustice inevitably contributes to and overlaps with other oppressions" using "the genre as a tool capable of expressing the complexity of black experience in America."[29]

In the final poem in the collection, entitled "Ceremony," Davenport highlights the songs, stories, "madness, voodoo & magic" that are not unique to New Orleans, but can be found in an abundance of places, including Soque Street, Georgia.[30] In "Mr. Papa Doc Williams (1877–1984)," Davenport gives voice to a ghost as dead Papa Doc Williams reflects on his life, including the time he and his family lived at 121 Soque Street, a haunted house. Yet as Doc contends, by the time the family reaches 121, they are tired of running, and ghosts are the least of their concerns. Before arriving in the community, Doc and his wife were persecuted because his wife was mistaken as a white woman, threats far more insidious than the ghosts they encounter at 121. To be sure, there are plenty of ghosts on Soque Street, a place where Doc remembers, "When they run off (or killed) all the Indians in Georgia, they started right/in on us!"[31] Soque Street is deeply haunted by this bloody history of colonization and slavery, with the speaker in "Ceremony for 103 Soque Street," highlighting that the Black families who live on a street with a Cherokee name, are "all the while, hainted."[32] Here the dead return and the community is often enveloped by a mysterious fog. The things forgotten or repressed, knowledge of shared bloodlines and histories of violent oppression, seethe, demanding recognition and calling for a reimagining of Appalachia as a historically diverse region.

As I outlined in the Introduction, to address that diversity Frank X Walker coined the term "Affrilachia," and in his poetry collection of the same name, he explains how the term celebrates Black culture and helps to draw attention to the parts of Appalachia that get lost between, "the dukes of hazard/and the beverly hillbillies."[33] He also moves in the collection between the horrors of the Middle Passage, slavery, segregation, the objectification and sexual violence against Black women, and the White-on-Black and Black-on-Black violence that often cuts young Black lives short. In "Amazin' Grace" Walker underlines the historic ruptures and acts of violence that have shaped Black lives, asking what prompted the change in John Newton, author of the Christian hymn, who transformed from slave ship captain to abolitionist. Was it, the poem asks, "the popping sound bloody flesh makes/when a sizzling branding iron" burns its mark onto human flesh?[34] The brutality of the Middle Passage is made manifest, ensuring that Newton is remembered first and foremost as a critical agent of the transatlantic slave trade. The rape of women on those slave ships casts a long, deep, threatening shadow that Walker explores as he examines the critical role of Black women's labor in "Statues of Liberty," the women who faced down "predators" in the workplace to "pave the way for a NOW," to give their children and grandchildren better opportunities.[35]

Yet Walker also laments the brutal violence that cuts short young Black lives in "Violins or Violen … ce," a poem that is also a plea for change. The brutal, bloody world that Walker depicts, in which young Black boys "claim their manhood early/because they might not be here" when they turn 18, tells a damning tale of how systemic racism, played out since slavery through segregation and urban and rural poverty, continues to haunt the present.[36] Walker's fears for the young are echoed in Ed Roberson's poem "Cascade," where the speaker takes stock of raising a daughter into adulthood, safely preventing his daughter from being a statistic: "the one more death/of a child shot by another, that reach of the street."[37] White spaces appear across "Cascade," creating moments for reflection as the poem moves between happy memories of a monster joke shared by father and daughter, and the specter of a different, more insidious, and menacing threat that reaches out from the streets. In these poems, Walker and Roberson dwell on street violence, police violence, White-on-Black and Black-on-Black violence, and child-against-child violence, all at once deeply uncanny and presenting views of an urban life that rarely feature in any of the region's stereotypes. Wester notes that recent Black American authors "especially toward the millennium's end, prove particularly critical of the ways blacks perpetuate oppression and violence among and against each other."[38] Walker and Roberson present Black-on-Black violence as part of the complex history of the Black American experience that has been riddled with brutality from the outset.

Black and Indigenous Appalachian writers have paved the way for critically reexamining Appalachia, putting the region's diversity and complexity front and center, which of course, also goes far beyond the experience of both groups, encompassing the plurality of a region also shaped by immigration since settler colonialism. Take, for example, poet Lisa Kwong who identifies as Appalasian, as an Asian from Appalachia. Born in Radford, Virginia to Chinese parents, Kwong writes in "This ABC (Appalachian-Born

Chinese Girl)" about growing up as a first-generation American with a "Southern accent" and all those "side-eyes Confederate flags who can't see/her Appalachian roots."[39] The idea of Appalachia as home is tempered by the hate-filled glances that seek to ostracize: if the stereotype of Appalachia depends on an idea of monolithic whiteness, within Appalachia certain individuals and communities also police ideas of belonging.

Korean-Appalachian Michael Croley, who I discussed in Chapter 2, reflects in his debut short story collection about complex attachments to small-town Appalachia. In the story "Slope," Wren Asher thinks about his Kentucky home, Fordyce, as the "bigoted place" where he and his Korean mother face all manner of stares and name-calling, the very title of the story a racist slur but one he never heard growing up because he "was constantly being called Japanese or Chinese [...] and later in middle school and high school, he was called *gook* and *chink*."[40] If home is that "bigoted place," then Wren finds life outside Kentucky much more accepting, although not without racial taunts and where he experiences a different form of othering, "marked more by his Kentucky accent and country sayings [...] People sometimes ask him to repeat what he says, as if he's a form of human entertainment and his speech has the quaint air of someone who is simple."[41] Both Kwong and Croley explore the haunting feelings that arise when questions of belonging are fraught and intensified by overt and casual racism.

The gothic helps to expose the multifarious nature of racism and inequality and importantly, the work of complicating and diversifying the region cannot rest only with those writing back at it: as Barbara Smith contends, Appalachian whiteness must also fully interrogate itself, recognizing its own complicity in racial oppression,[42] the side of Appalachia that Ann Pancake rails against in her "Letter to West Virginia, November 2016": in the wake of Trump's election win she acknowledges that alongside her love for her homeplace, she also hates it "when our culture is narrow, intolerant."[43] Without question, the 45th president has enraged Appalachian authors and promoted deep levels of self-interrogation, and David Joy's *Those We Thought We Knew* (2023) pushes for the form of racial reckoning that Smith calls for.[44]

In the opening line, "The graves took all night to dig," Joy places the gothic front and center of his searing expose of racism both beyond and within Appalachia.[45] Young, Black artist and activist, Toya Gardner, rails against historic and contemporary injustices: the graves at the start of the novel are part of Toya's illicit art installation on a college campus to draw attention to what the college moved to build Robertson Hall. As she explains, "They bulldozed a Cherokee mound and razed a Black church," both rendered throw-away.[46] Toya's grandmother, Vess, remembers the stories people told about the disinterred: "Faces drawn back to skeletons, hands drawn back to bones," all "parts of broken stories" Vess has carried "all her life like thorns," sharp reminders about the ways Black bodies are viewed and treated across U.S. history.[47]

Toya will not be silenced in her attempts to bring forward a full reckoning, and for challenging racism wherever she finds it, from Civil War monuments to its more insidious, everyday forms, she is murdered. The rest of the novel focuses on bringing her killer to justice and finding the Klan members who violently beat Deputy Ernie Allison, both events pointing to the different ways racism operates. The febrile atmosphere and levels of overt racial hatred in the novel are partly attributed to the election of Donald Trump: the boys that disturb Toya's vigil drive a loud "Dodge diesel" with two flags, one "an American flag with a cross centered between two assault rifles, the words, GOD, GUNS, TRUMP written along the top and bottom," embodying the increased confidence of the far-right in the wake of the 2016 presidential election. Yet in no way does Trump's presidency alone account for the levels of racism that run throughout the novel: Joy demands consideration of the insidious and structural racism that has underpinned American society across history.[48] As a result, Joy importantly resists employing the Ku Klux Klan character, William Dean Cawthorn, as Toya's killer. Instead, the town's Sheriff, John Coggins, a supposedly longtime friend of Toya's grandparents, especially her deceased grandfather, Lon, is cast in that role.

Joy does not seek to diminish the threat posed by the Ku Klux Klan, but rather to intensify it: Cawthorn could easily have been Toya's killer, but as detective Leah Green discovers when she arrests Cawthorn and finds a book full of local Klan member details, "it was the ones we thought we knew, those were the ones who broke our hearts."[49] If Cawthorn represents overt, unabashed racism, then the Sheriff embodies covert and systemic racism, and it is vital that Toya dies at his hands to underscore the violence intrinsic to racism, however it manifests. While the Sheriff's eventual death marks the end of one monster, given all the names in Cawthorn's book, it does not mark the end of the structural racism from which he fed.

As a white writer, Joy's exposure of Appalachian and American racism challenges the region and nation to recognize their own prejudices, but the region's non-white writers lead the way in shifting the dial for a full acknowledgment of Appalachia's diversity. Necessarily replete with gothic tropes, the region's Black, Indigenous, immigrant, and first-generation literature ensures that racist horror is held up and exposed in all its forms and brutality, even as they underscore their deeply felt connections to Appalachia, however complex those attachments may be.

While bell hooks identified neither as an Appalachian nor Affrilachian writer, the Kentucky-born author claimed "a solidarity, a sense of belonging" that connected her "with the Appalachian past" of her ancestors "black, Native American, white."[50] Across the poems in *Appalachian Elegy*, hooks writes extensively about listening to the voices of the dead because while, as she writes in poem 4, the earth "is all at once a grave," it is also a "bed of new beginnings."[51] Is it at once deeply haunted, a place seething with ghosts and a landscape destroyed by war and an extractive logic, but also a site for renewal. In the collection, hooks gives form to many of the region's ghosts, but she also seeks to move beyond that haunting, to be always informed by it, but not shaped by it. Resisting and pushing back against labels defined hooks and her writing, and as a self-identified queer author who at one time labeled herself "queer-pas-gay," hooks lived her life at a critical intersection of race, class, gender, and sexuality.

While hooks embraced intersectionality, she also cautioned that "White people, gay and straight, could show greater understanding of the impact of racial oppression on people of color by not attempting to make these oppressions synonymous, but rather by showing the ways they are linked but differ," and much of the work undertaken in LGBTQ+ studies seeks not to easily elide race, gender, and sexuality but to understand these intersecting issues in their complexity.[52] As Siobhan Somerville outlines, "queer approaches make visible broad variations of sexual practice and self-understanding in various historical and cultural contexts" and move beyond "anachronistic" notions of "sexual identity."[53] "Queer Appalachia" is an area of critical study that seeks to further expand the understanding of LGBTQ+ experiences through the lens of place, or as Z. Zane McNeil puts it, "the more I've considered what makes me queer, the more I have questioned if Appalachia itself is a *queered* place—a region rendered deviant through the lenses of the opioid crisis, poverty, and environmental degradation."[54] Their recognition of the challenges of being "queer" in a deeply othered region highlights the many questions posed in Appalachian LGBTQ+ literature.

LGBTQ+ Rights and Appalachian Gothic Literature

Laura Westengard proposes that "twentieth- and twenty-first century U.S. queer culture is gothic at the core" and that "queer culture that responds to and challenges traumatic marginalization" does so "by creating a distinctly gothic rhetoric and aesthetic."[55] The gothic is vital to understanding LGBTQ+ characters and their struggles, struggles intensified in an already othered Appalachia. For Allison Carey, many LGBTQ+ authors "and their work have been doubly erased: disregarded within the literature of the United States because they're Appalachian [...] and overlooked (or excluded from) the Appalachian literary tradition because they are queer."[56] Carey examines

LGBTQ+ literature since the early twentieth century, turning back to writers such as James Still who "adamantly denied being gay until the end of his life," but whose "sexuality has been a topic of discussion among scholars," through to self-identifying LGBTQ+ writers in the twenty-first century who include Fenton Johnson, Dorothy Allison, Silas House, Carter Sickels, Mesha Maren, Jonathan Corcoran, Rahul Mehta, R. K. Fauth, and Neema Avashia.[57] Throughout their writing, these authors grapple with the question posed by Glasby, Gradin, and Ryerson: "What weight is born by being both queer and Appalachian?"[58] LGBTQ+ Appalachian writers wrestle with this and several other challenges, including the complexities of being rendered other in an already othered place.

Gothic tropes abound as authors depict LGBTQ+ Appalachian characters and their struggles to navigate their sexuality in often rural, deeply religious communities that harbor varying strains of anti-LGBTQ+ sentiment that are not unique to Appalachia but are felt particularly acutely in small, rural, often religiously conservative communities, or what Paulina Palmer terms "the oppressive climate of rural America."[59] In her memoir, *Another Appalachia* (2022), Neema Avashia, who self-identifies as a "queer desi Appalachian woman," writes about growing up in 1980s Appalachia as a first-generation Indian American, and being "the only Hindu in church camps full of Christians"[60] and gay in a place where "I never knew anyone [...] who was openly gay. It wasn't a topic discussed [...] We played Smear the Queer in my street, throwing one another down a grassy hill, without ever questioning the name of the game."[61] Even today, and especially in the wake of Trump's election in 2016, when Avashia returns to West Virginia, she does not take her wife along on certain visits to the people that she knew growing up because she still does not know if they will be welcomed and accepted. She writes, "West Virginia is the only home I know, though it is not a home that always loves me back."[62] In Appalachian literature, those people who would be rendered monstrous by anti-LGBTQ+ sentiment are depicted in all their complexity and humanity, while those who label, ostracize and prohibit, driven by fear and/or outright prejudice, take on terrifying forms.

Fellow West Virginian, and first-generation South Asian author, Rahul Mehta, writes extensively about Appalachia in their fiction and poetry. Their recent poetry collection, *Feeding the Ghosts* (2024), is a deeply personal book in which Mehta explores the ways they still struggle with the past, of "growing up brown, the child of immigrants, and queer in West Virginia."[63] In their first novel, *No Other World* (2017), set in rural, western New York and India, Mehta depicts the struggles of Kiran Shah, an Indian American gay man struggling with his sexual identity in the late 1980s to the late 1990s, and who internalizes the demonized narratives surrounding LGBTQ+ people generated during the AIDS crisis. He sees himself as "Irradiated, toxic [...] He couldn't risk contaminating his family."[64] Later, living in New York and starting to embrace his sexuality, he is spotted by a cousin who cannot believe what he sees:

> the figure he would believe was Kiran would be swathed in a gold sari—not *swathed*, because swathed means enveloped, swathed means cocooned, and this figure would be neither. His midriff would be bare and the sleeves of his blouse very short; there would be gold metal bands wrapped snakelike around his upper arms, and though it would be dark, the cousin would notice, as the figure passed beneath a streetlamp, that his skin was shimmering with body glitter.[65]

Here, Kiran's cousin is unable to reconcile his idea of Kiran with the person he sees on the street because his cousin measures Kiran through the lens of heteronormativity, seeing his cousin as monstrous, frightful. As a result, the cousins "turn away from one another, and this pattern would continue for almost two decades."[66]

After a mental health crisis, a trip to India where Kiran befriends Pooja, a hijra, a transgender teenage girl comfortable with her body and sexuality in ways that surprise Kiran who has lived so much of his life in hiding, and a brutal fight with his cousin Bharat that results in Kiran's hospitalization, the love that pours to him from the rest of his family makes him reassess "his own armor, the walls he'd erected, the way he'd betrayed and repeatedly pushed his family away. And yet they'd all come. Even his cousin-brothers abroad had made calls and sent cards."[67] The family's gradual acceptance of Kiran's identity sees Mehta underscoring love and understanding at the close of the novel, with Kiran finding ways to be himself and no longer having to hide in the shadows.

The resolution that Kiran finds is not always secured for LGBTQ+ characters, especially in the literature published after Trump's election win in 2016 and the threats posed to LGBTQ+ rights. Since 2016, "hostile rhetoric and conspiracy theories [...] aimed at transgender and nonbinary people" in particular, are on the rise in the United States,[68] and in April 2023, CNN reported that at "least 417 anti-LGBTQ bills have been introduced in state legislatures across the United States since the start of the year—a new record, according to American Civil Liberties Union data as of April 3."[69] Indeed, Glasby, Gradin, and Ryerson ask, "What might it mean to live or write as queer in Appalachia after the 2016 election process, the results of which seem to have ushered in a new sense of vulnerability and fear for many LGBTQ+ persons (who might also be undocumented, of color, disabled, and/or Muslim)?"[70] An increasing number of Appalachian authors and texts exploring LGBTQ+ lives are pushing back against the backdrop of rising hostility toward the LGBTQ+ community.

In the region's LGBTQ+ literature and poetry published since 2016, gothic tropes proliferate. Several authors and poets overtly talk back to Trump, naming and shaming him at various turns, whereas others write back in less overt ways, appealing in their depictions of LGBTQ+ crises for kindness and understanding in a historical moment when equal rights seem far from secure and hatred dominates right-wing rhetoric. Against that background, doris davenport writes "Halloween 2017" a political poem capturing the shift in mood as Trump's Republican Party took major steps to the extreme right, highlighting the sense of outrage and the feeling of being "terrorized" by the changing political landscape and what it portends for anyone who does not conform to extreme Republican norms.[71]

Mesha Maren's two novels to date seethe with the difficulties of exploring and accepting LGBTQ+ identities. At the start of her first novel, *Sugar Run*, that I also discussed in Chapter 2, central protagonist Jodi McCarty is released from prison in Georgia having served a life sentence for killing her girlfriend, Paula in 1989, when Jodi was only 17. The novel alternates between Jodi meeting Paula in 1988 and the events leading up to Paula's death, and Jodi's post-prison life in 2007 where she eventually returns home to West Virginia, with a new love, Miranda. Back when Jodi found herself in love with Paula, she thinks, "If she could push back the words—dyke, queer—then everything would make sense and turn out all right. Sometimes, though, the terror of it grips her, the knowledge that she is not seen at all, or seen only backward and out of focus. It is a feeling she is sure will crush her someday."[72] Here the terrible power of homophobic words and the failure to see the humanity of LGBTQ+ people is a weight that threatens to extinguish Jodie. By the time she returns to West Virginia, those feelings, that pervasive sense of terror still resides, and when her brother Dennis asks Jodie if she and Miranda are having sex, "there was a flint edge" to his voice "that buried itself deep inside Jodi." Her feelings of dread are compounded by his overt homophobia, asking if they have "some kind of sick shit going on," reiterating that "I can't stand to think of those boys growing up around something sick like that," after which he "dragged his eyes up and down Jodi's body." His hostile gaze reinforces Jodie's worst fears, yet Maren does not solely locate this hostility toward the LGBTQ+ community in conservative communities in Appalachia: in her most recent novel, *Perpetual West* (2022), set across Appalachia, Texas, and Mexico, life for LGBTQ+ people remains precarious especially, although not exclusively, in heavily religious, conservative places.[73]

In her poetry collection WWJD (2019), Savannah Sipple explores what it means to be a queer woman in a deeply religious Appalachian community in poems that resound with love of place and hatred of place, the desire to leave and the desire to stay, a complex collection where violence, religion, self-harm, body dysmorphia, and love coalesce. In a direct shot at Trump, in "When Those Who Have the Power Start to Lose It, They Panic," Sipple explores misogyny and how the reward for continually demeaning women includes being "elected President."[74] Sipple also considers the horrors of being trapped by narratives about weight, sexuality, and religion, to name just a few, and her poems work through these difficult challenges to a place of full and unwavering self-acceptance. In "What We Tell Ourselves," the speaker works through a love/hate relationship with Appalachia, where to leave is to breathe, to be able to be yourself without the judgment of the church and a close-minded community where "When it all goes to hell, the holiest/among them turn on you first."[75] Rejection by church and community centers on what Justin Ray Dutton argues are the particular links between "queerphobia" and the region's Christianity. While acknowledging that Appalachia is no more Christian than any other part of the United States, nor is it exclusively Christian, Dutton discusses what he calls "Appalachian Christian queerphobic rhetoric (ACQR)," a rhetoric that "panoptically enforces toxic rhetoric and realities."[76] In the poems across *WWJD*, Sipple works through her complex relationship with her evangelical faith and her own personal relationship with Jesus. In her poems, many with Jesus in the title, including "Jesus and I went to the Walmart" and "Jesus Signs Me Up for a Dating App," Sipple presents a Jesus who loves all, pushing back against those in her own faith or other faiths that use religion to promote anti-LGBTQ+ sentiment.

Similarly, Silas House explores religion and homosexuality in *Southernmost* (2018), where in a small town in Tennessee the evangelical pastor, Asher Sharp, is rejected by his congregation and his wife when he stands up for two gay men, having worked through his own religious hatred toward LGBTQ+ people which previously led him to join his mother in renouncing his gay brother.[77] The novel begins in 2015 against the backdrop of the Supreme Court's ruling that states must allow and recognize same-sex marriages. In a complex series of events that sees Asher voted out from his pastorship, his delivery of an impassioned sermon preaching love and kindness, and the loss of custody of his nine-year-old son, Justin, Asher kidnaps Justin and flees to Key West where he hopes to find his brother. On the drive to Key West, and when he, his brother, and Justin return to Tennessee when Asher decides to turn himself in, the road signs loom large, warning that Appalachia and the wider South are hostile territory. Sign after sign a scathing reminder that places across the region still hold firmly to the confederate flag, "THIS FLAG IS

HERITAGE, NOT HATE" and specifically promote anti-LGBTQ+ hate, with signs such as "GOD HATES FAGS" and "GAY IS NOT OKAY" monstrously reminding passersby that alongside "JAM JELLY MOLASSES" and "BEST PEACHES 4 MILES," the region serves up fire and brimstone warnings about so-called sinners with its slices of hospitality.[78]

Insidious hatred toward the LGBTQ+ community is compounded by racial hatred in Halle Hill's short story "Bitch Baby" (2023) where gay, transvestite Reggie is met with vicious brutality when he and his sister, Celine, are pulled over by the police at a moment when Reggie is wearing a "magnificent dress" that "glittered all over him."[79] Celine narrates the story, and aware of the fate of others who crossed societal definitions of sexual propriety, she shares her perpetual worry that Reggie might end up "stripped naked, black and blue, and hung from a tree."[80] All Reggie's dreams of escaping the conservative confines of their community come crashing down during the violent encounter with the police officer. Celine watches on in horror, seeing her brother "laying on the road, gashes, all over," the police officer inflicting blow after blow before delivering his parting message to Celine: "'Leave it and drive on,' the officer said. 'Unless you want a turn, too.' He spit at the ground beside us, turned, and drove away."[81] The story offers a searing reminder that while all members of the LGBTQ+ community face violent bigotry, the racial hatred continually stoked by the far-right produces a compounded threat to the LGBTQ+ BIPOC community.

The increased venom toward the LGBTQ+ community runs throughout *Lovesick Blossoms* (2023), by prominent LGBTQ+ Appalachian author Julia Watts. In the novel, the words of Justice Clarence Thomas reverberate with dread:[82] after overturning *Roe v. Wade* in 2022, Thomas wrote the Supreme Court "should reconsider all of its 'substantive due process precedents,' including Lawrence v. Texas, the 2003 decision that established the right to same-sex intimacy, and Obergefell v. Hodges, which legalized same-sex marriage in 2015."[83] While Watt's most recent novel is primarily set in 1950s Kentucky, with a small section at the close that brings events up to the 1970s, twenty-first-century threats to LGBTQ+ rights cast a shadowy presence over events. When Samuel and Frances meet at an academic soiree for their respective husbands, the two women, neither one who fits in with the other wives, form an immediate friendship before quickly falling in love.[84]

It is Frances's young daughter, Susan, who discovers Samuel and Frances in bed together after their desire for each other becomes too confined in the hidden, windowless space of France's pantry. When Susan discovers them: "Samuel's expression was instantly readable. It was abject terror."[85] Terror and fear dominate the novel from this moment. When their affair is eventually discovered by Frances's husband, Henry, himself a serial philanderer,

Frances takes too many Valium pills and Henry sends her to *Our Lady of the Peace*, a psychiatric hospital where lobotomies and electroshock therapy are the order of the day not only for patients with mental health conditions, but also those deemed sexual "deviants," who face this monstrous, medical form of conversion therapy. When Samuel thinks about *Frankenstein*, "She wondered if there was any member of an outcast group who read *Frankenstein* without thinking, *the monster is me*."[86] Just as Mary Shelley's *Frankenstein* rests "on a false perception" that "construes the creature as a 'monster'," so Watts represents the monstrous not as those who do not conform to societal norms and standards, but rather those who enforce those standards, from the law and medical professions to every day society and its own policing of "decency" and the borders between in- and out-groups.[87] As Henry tells Frances, his own infidelity is "a perfectly normal temptation that would've been equally tempting to any other healthy male adult,"[88] his association of "normal" and "healthy" rendering Frances abnormal and unhealthy.

Once released from the psychiatric hospital, Henry takes Frances home and in bed, in one of the most realistic and gothic moments in the novel, "before Frances could process what was happening, her nightgown was up around her waist, and he was on her, then in her. She closed her eyes and tried to act her part."[89] Henry's ownership over Frances is made more horrific given an earlier scene in the novel where Frances awkwardly tries to insert a diaphragm because she bears sole responsibility for birth control: having signed off on Frances's incarceration and conversion therapy, Henry violently reasserts heteronormativity without any consideration of consent or birth control, and his aggressiveness starkly contrasts the tenderness and passion Samuel and Frances experienced in the same space.

Watts ends her novel 18 years later, with Frances and Samuel finding each other again in New York, both single and having successfully pursued writing careers. The emphasis on how times change both simultaneously provides Frances and Samuel with opportunities to spend the rest of their lives together, but also carries the looming threats to equal rights represented by Donald Trump, the hundreds of state bills to limit LGBTQ+ freedoms, and Justice Clarence Thomas's threat to hard-won equal rights. In an interview, Watts makes clear that she "started dreaming up *Lovesick Blossoms* in the fateful year of 2016" and that while "Trans youth are probably the most vulnerable […] in this climate, none of us is truly safe."[90] In this period of deep uncertainty and hatred, the gothic will continue to recur across Appalachian LGBTQ+ fiction to represent past injustices and record the ongoing battles for LGBTQ+ equality: the "queer uncanny," as Palmer defines it, has much still to do.

Notes

1. Goddu, *Gothic America*, 7–8.
2. Glasby, Gradin, and Ryerson, "Introduction," 1.
3. McCollum, "Introduction," 2.
4. Ibid., 2.
5. Turner, "Introduction," xvii–xviii.
6. Perdue, "Red and Black in the Southern Appalachians," 23.
7. Blethen, "Pioneer Settlement," 17.
8. Anderson and Benson Taylor, "Letting the Other Story Go," 75.
9. Hausman was born in Michigan and is a citizen of the Cherokee Nation of Oklahoma. He mainly grew up in North Carolina and Georgia.
10. Hausman, *Riding the Trail of Tears*.
11. Clapsaddle, *Even As We Breathe*.
12. Hausman, 13.
13. Ibid., 14.
14. Ibid., 6.
15. Ibid., 33.
16. Ibid., 63.
17. Ibid., 232.
18. Friedman, "Illegible Histories, Invisible Movements," 91.
19. Hausman, 279.
20. Crowe, *Radiogenesis: Poems 1986-2006*, 12.
21. Locklear, "Not Either/Or, But Both: Cherokee and Appalachian Identity in Annette Saunooke Clapsaddle's *Even As We Breathe*," 34.
22. Clapsaddle, 27.
23. Burnham, "Is There an Indigenous Gothic?" 227.
24. Ibid., 210.
25. Ibid., 229–230.
26. Locklear, 39.
27. Davenport, *Madness Like Morning Glories*.
28. Davenport, "Cycles and (Scrambled) Seasons," 334.
29. Wester, *African American Gothic*, 256.
30. Davenport, *madness like morning glories*, 58.
31. Ibid., 41–42.
32. Ibid., 21.
33. Walker, *Affrilachia*, 93.
34. Ibid., 59.
35. Ibid., 12.
36. Ibid., 40.
37. Roberson, *Asked What Has Changed*, 54.
38. Wester, 254.
39. Kwong, *Becoming Appalasian*, 8.
40. Croley, *Any Other Place*, 9.
41. Ibid., 5.
42. Smith, "De-gradations of Whiteness."
43. Ann Pancake, "Letter to West Virginia, November 2016," 241.
44. Joy, *Those We Thought We Knew*.
45. Ibid., 3.

46 Ibid., 29.
47 Ibid., 50.
48 Ibid., 194.
49 Ibid., 297.
50 hooks, bell, *Appalachian Elegy: Poetry and Place*, 4. Copyright © 2012 Gloria Jean Watkins (bell hooks). Reprinted by permission of The University Press of Kentucky.
51 Ibid., "4", 14.
52 hooks, *Talking Back*, 125.
53 Somerville, "Introduction," 5.
54 McNeil, "Introduction," 1.
55 Westengard, *Gothic Queer Culture*, 3.
56 Carey, *Doubly Erased*, 17.
57 Ibid., 31.
58 Glasby, Gradin, and Ryerson, 1.
59 Palmer, *The Queer Uncanny*, 116.
60 Avashia, *Another Appalachia*, 155
61 Ibid., 57.
62 Ibid., 92.
63 Mehta, *Feeding the Ghosts*, xii.
64 Rahul Mehta, *No Other World*, 206.
65 Ibid., 185.
66 Ibid., 186.
67 Ibid., 282.
68 Walters, "Kamala Harris Warns of Threats to LGBTQ+ Rights during Visit to Stonewall."
69 Choi, "Record Number of Anti-LGBTQ Bills have been Introduced this Year."
70 Glasby, Gradin, and Ryerson, 1.
71 Davenport, "Halloween 2017," 58.
72 Maren, *Sugar Run*, 60.
73 Maren, *Perpetual West*.
74 Sipple, *WWJD and other poems*, 19.
75 Ibid., 27.
76 Dutton, "Challenging Dominant Christianity's Queerphobic Rhetoric," 37.
77 Silas House, *Southernmost*.
78 Ibid., 141 and 322.
79 Hill, *Good Women*, 131.
80 Ibid., 126.
81 Ibid., 132.
82 Watts, *Lovesick Blossoms*.
83 Moreau, "How will Roe v. Wade Reversal Affect LGBTQ Rights? Experts, Advocates Weigh in."
84 Watts, 36.
85 Ibid., 162.
86 Ibid., 168.
87 Smith, *Gothic Literature*, 45.
88 Watts, 241.
89 Ibid., 313.
90 Watts, "Author Interview: Julia Watts."

Conclusion

Appalachia has played a critical role in the growth and progress of the national economy, but its gothic literature demands pause, time to question the costs of a relentless pursuit of growth, from the forced removal of Indigenous people to slavery, and from coal mining to the climate crisis. Of course, the climate crisis is arguably the most existential threat, and pushing beyond the term Anthropocene, Botting coins the term "Monstrocene" to encompass the human and non-human terrors and horrors of the climate crisis. Yet Botting cautions against the pitfalls of dark ecology and a tendency to frame the climate crisis in purely monstrous terms, concerned that climate monsters may "only serve to horrify and paralyze all thought, all imagination, all response."[1] However, in a region rendered monstrous in the popular imagination, Appalachian authors must turn to the monstrous, not to "paralyze," but to expose the monster for what it really is and in the case of the climate crisis, the monster is partly formed by the waves of fossil fuel extraction that have wreaked destruction across the region.

The critical reflections on an extractive logic across Appalachian gothic literature are a repeated refrain, a ballad about the destruction of place and the devastating costs to the humans and non-humans. Sharae Deckard reminds us "capitalism is always in search of new commodity frontiers for extraction and appropriation," and the alternate energy demands of the green transition continue to demand extraction.[2] The lithium required especially for "electric vehicles and battery manufacturing" means the "demand for lithium" just in the United States, "is expected to grow more than six times by […] the end of the decade."[3] This demand is generating a new boom in Appalachian areas rich in lithium reserves: the federal government as well as several companies are investing in battery factories and electric car plants in the region.[4] In economically depressed communities the prospect of new jobs as part of the green transition is vital, but in a region where extraction has come at great costs to the health of the environment and residents, there are grave concerns about the destructive impacts of this latest turn to Appalachia as a natural resource to be harnessed for the greater good. The question remains about whether the green transition can approach extraction any differently, especially when it is driven largely by the private sector. The Appalachian gothic, in its representation of deep coal mining, MTR and fracking, is riddled with extractive horrors, and if newer forms of extraction continue to exploit people and place, then the Appalachian gothic will continue to be critical for the region's authors as they work through the complex machinations of life, human and non-human, in a sacrifice zone, their contribution sitting alongside the extensive grassroots activism in Appalachia that has long fought back against socioeconomic and environmental injustice.

While an extractive logic is a central, urgent aspect of the Appalachian gothic, the Appalachian gothic is not merely a tale of extractivism. Contemporary gothic Appalachian literature helps to expose several other regional and national concerns, including the post-Trump moment that I discussed in Chapters 2 and 3. The post-Trump moment in Appalachian literature continues to have a palpable presence and Julia Franks's *The Say So* (2023) is a recent example. The novel explores the question of choice in relation to abortion and adoption since the 1950s, with characters grappling at different historical junctures with questions of choice, and they carry their decisions "through the corridors of everyday life, hallways so narrow they held no room for the unsayable, the monstrous, or surreal."[5] Drawing on her own experiences of giving her son up for adoption when she was a college student, and propelled by Trump's appointments to the Supreme Court, Franks recalls the horrors women experienced before safe abortions were made available to all American women in 1973.

Franks reminds us that in the pre-*Roe v. Wade* era, huge numbers of women who felt forced into "performing the procedure upon themselves," bled "to death on the weekends."[6] This deeply gothic image of women's bodies bleeding out serves as a stark reminder of what is at stake in a period where so many states across the United States impose bans and/or restrictions on women's bodily autonomy in the wake of the Supreme Court's ruling in *Dobbs v. Jackson* on June 24, 2022.

While references to various presidents and politicians, notably John F. Kennedy, Lydon B. Johnson, and Robert F. Kennedy, can be found across Appalachian fiction, the post-Trump moment in Appalachian literature is shaped by palpable levels of anger and fear shared by several contemporary authors and poets. Frank X Walker is outraged by Trump across the poems in *Masked Man, Black*, referring to Trump in "Bad Medicine" as the "Commander-in-Cheat" who cannot be trusted to keep the nation safe, especially its most vulnerable citizens,[7] and in "Rainy Days," Nikki Giovanni associates dark skies with the fact that "donald trump/must be president."[8] This fervent need to speak out against Trump also forms the basis of Mark

Powell's latest novel, *The Late Rebellion*, a novel he felt compelled to write after Trump's 2016 win. He describes the book as "a dark family comedy set in the Appalachian South that I know—a place that is far more diverse and complex than generally presented."[9] Against a backdrop of a changed world in Germantown, South Carolina, where "MAGA stickers" revitalize "rebel flags," family is complicated.[10] In a novel that largely revolves around its central family and its various crises, Powell gives voice to several other characters in the wider community to establish the fear and trepidation about the current state of the nation. Those voices include first-generation Nayma González, whose childhood and young adulthood are shaped by her family's experiences of immigration, including "The hassles from ICE" and the "rhetoric of hate—*build a wall! build a wall!*" that is "spouted by the same folks paying you three dollars an hour to pick their tomatoes or change their babies."[11] The novel makes messy the things that polarized political debates want to simply bracket and control.

The post-Trump moment in Appalachian literature exposes some of the most acute crises facing the region and the nation, with Appalachian writers not shrinking from engaging with racism and anti-LGBTQ+ sentiments that are monstrous but are unique neither to Appalachia nor the South. Arthur F. Redding argues "Contemporary gothic is […] a cultural formation specific to the perceived acceleration of catastrophe within American life. It speaks to and of our unhinging, our precarious condition today," and contemporary Appalachian gothic literature seethes with that precariousness, whether it takes the form of racism and the threats to LGBTQ+ people in an already othered region, or the climate crisis that brings about a stark reckoning with life in the Anthropocene.[12] Naturally, these concerns are shared by the southern and American gothic, but they shape a growing and repeated refrain across contemporary Appalachian literature, a body of literature infused with gothic tropes as it responds to how others see the region and reveals the nuanced, diverse, and complex Appalachia that has always existed. The inability to see beyond stereotypes of the region comes from an unwillingness to see the monstrous in all its reality, a reality that gothic Appalachian literature continues to expose.

Notes

1. Botting, "Monstrocene," 319.
2. Deckard, "Uncanny States," 178.
3. See Reuters, "Global Demand for Lithium Batteries to Leap Five-Fold by 2023—Li Bridge."
4. See Kaufmann's "The Lithium War Next Door."
5. Franks, *The Say So*, 269.

6 Ibid., 50.
7 Walker, *Masked Man, Black: Pandemic and Protest Poems*, 6.
8 Giovanni, *Make Me Rain: Poems and Prose*, 86.
9 Regal House Publishing's "Mark Powell."
10 Powell, *The Late Rebellion*, 20.
11 Ibid., 62–63.
12 Redding, *Haints*, 9.

Works Cited

Althofer, Jayson and Brian Musgrove. "'A Ghost in Daylight': Drugs and the Horror of Modernity." *Palgrave Communications* 4, no. 112 (September 2018): 1–11. https://doi.org/10.1057/s41599-018-0162-0.
Anderson, Eric Gary, Taylor Hagood and Daniel Cross Turner. Introduction to *Undead Souths: The Gothic and Beyond in Southern Literature and Culture*, edited by Eric Gary Anderson, Taylor Hagood, and Daniel Cross Turner, 1–9. Baton Rouge: Louisiana State University Press, 2015.
Anderson, Eric Gary and Melanie Benson Taylor. "Letting the Other Story Go: The Native South in and beyond the Anthropocene." *Native South* 12 (2019): 74–98. https://www.proquest.com/scholarly-journals/letting-other-story-go-native-south-beyond/docview/2327839863/se-2.
Appalachian Citizens' Law Center. "Estill County Radioactive Fracking Waste." Accessed July 5, 2023. https://aclc.org/environmental-justice/estill-county-fracking-waste/.
Arnow, Harriette. *The Dollmaker*. London: Vintage, 2017. First published 1954 by Macmillan (New York).
Attaway, William. *Blood on the Forge*. New York: The New York Review of Books, 2005. First published 1941 by Doubleday Doran (New York).
Avashia, Neema. *Another Appalachia: Coming Up Queer and Indian in a Mountain Place*. Morgantown: West Virginia University Press.
Batteau, Allen W., ed. *Appalachia and America: Autonomy and Regional Dependence*. Lexington: The University Press of Kentucky, 1983.
———. *The Invention of Appalachia*. Tucson: The University of Arizona Press, 1990.
Benedict, Laura. *Devil's Oven*. Gallowstree Press, 2012.
Billings, Dwight B. "Once Upon a Time in 'Trumpalachia': *Hillbilly Elegy*, Personal Choice, and the Blame Game." In *Appalachian Reckoning: A Region Responds to Hillbilly Elegy*, edited by Anthony Harkins and Meredith McCarroll, 38–59. Morgantown: West Virginia University Press, 2019.
Billings, Dwight B., Gurney Norman and Katherine Ledford, ed. *Back Talk from Appalachia: Confronting Stereotypes*. Lexington: The University Press of Kentucky, 1999.
Billings, Dwight B. and Kathleen M. Blee. *The Road to Poverty: The Making of Wealth and Hardship in Appalachia*. Cambridge: Cambridge University Press, 2000.
Black, Brian. *Petrolia: The Landscape of America's First Oil Boom*. Baltimore: The Johns Hopkins University Press, 2000.
Blethen, H. Tyler. "Pioneer Settlement." In *High Mountains Rising: Appalachia in Time and Place*, edited by Richard A. Straw and H. Tyler Blethen, 17–29. Urbana: University of Illinois Press, 2004.

Botting, Fred. *Gothic*, 2nd ed. London: Routledge, 2014.
———. "Monstrocene." In *Dark Scenes from Damaged Earth*, edited by Justin D. Edwards, Rune Graulund, and Johan Höglund, 314–337. Minneapolis: The University of Minnesota Press, 2022.
Braudy, Leo. *Haunted: On Ghosts, Witches, Vampires, Zombies, and Other Monsters of the Natural and Supernatural Worlds*. New Haven: Yale University Press, 2016.
Brinkmeyer, Jr. Robert H. "Discovering Gold in the Back of Beyond: The Fiction of Ron Rash." Review of *Nothing Gold Can Stay* by Ron Rash. *The Virginia Quarterly Review* 89, no. 3 (Summer 2013): 219–223. https:www.jstor.org/stable/26447072.
Brown, Karida L. *Gone Home: Race and Roots through Appalachia*. Chapel Hill: The University of North Carolina Press, 2018.
Brown, Taylor. *Gods of Howl Mountain*. New York: Picador, 2019. First published 2018 by St Martin's Press (New York).
Burgess, Shawn. *The Tear Collector*. RhetAskew Publishing, 2019.
———. *Ghosts of Grief Hollow*. RhetAskew Publishing, 2022.
Burnham, Michelle. "Is There an Indigenous Gothic?" In *A Companion to American Gothic*, edited by Charles L. Crow, 225–237. Chichester: John Wiley & Sons, 2014.
Butler, Tom and George Wuerthner, ed. *Plundering Appalachia: The Tragedy of Mountaintop-Removal Coal Mining*. San Rafael: Earth Aware, 2009.
Carey, Allison E. *Doubly Erased: LGBTQ Literature in Appalachia*. New York: State University of New York Press, 2023.
Case, Anne and Angus Deaton. *Deaths of Despair and the Future of Capitalism*. Princeton: Princeton University Press 2020.
Castro, Joy. *Flight Risk*. Seattle: Lake Union, 2021.
Catte, Elizabeth. *What You Are Getting Wrong About Appalachia*. Cleveland: Belt Publishing, 2018.
———. "Why 'Trump Country isn't as Republican as you Think." *The Guardian*, February 22, 2019. https://www.theguardian.com/news/2019/feb/22/trump-country-republican-appalachia-virginia-activism.
Choi, Annette. "Record Number of anti-LGBTQ Bills have been Introduced this Year." *CNN*, April 6, 2023. https://edition.cnn.com/2023/04/06/politics/anti-lgbtq-plus-state-bill-rights-dg/index.html.
Claborn, John. "From Black Marxism to Industrial Ecosystem: Racial and Ecological Crisis in William Attaway's *Blood on the Forge*." *Modern Fiction Studies* 55, no. 3 (2009): 578–579. https://www.jstor.org/stable/26287371.
Clines, Francis X. "Flooding in Appalachia Stirs Outrage Over a Mining Method." *The New York Times*, August 12, 2002. https://www.nytimes.com/2002/08/12/us/flooding-in-appalachia-stirs-outrage-over-a-mining-method.html.
Cobb, James C. Afterword: Searching for Southern Identity to *A Companion to the Literature and Culture of the American South*, edited by Richard Gray and Owen Robinson, 591–607. Oxford: Blackwell Publishing, 2007. First published 2004 by Blackwell (Oxford).
Cooper, Lydia R. "McCarthy, Tennessee, and the Southern Gothic." In *The Cambridge Companion to Cormac McCarthy*, edited by Steven Frye, 41–53. Cambridge: Cambridge University Press, 2013.
Crane, David M. "Alice in Wonderland: Atrocity and Accountability in the 21st Century, A World Turned Upside Down." *Washington University Global Studies Law Review* 21, no. 1 (January 1, 2022): 33–46. https://journals.library.wustl.edu/globalstudies/article/id/8720/.

Croley, Michael. *Any Other Place: Stories*. Durham: Blair Press, 2019.
Crowe, Thomas Rain. *Radiogenesis: Poems 1986-2006*. Charlotte: Main Street Rag, 2007.
davenport, doris. *madness like morning glories*. Baton Rouge: Louisiana State University Press, 2005.
———. "Cycles and (Scrambled) Seasons." In *Mountains Piled upon Mountains*, edited by Jessica Corey, 276. Morgantown: West Virginia University Press, 2019.
———. "Halloween 2017." In *LGBTQ Fiction and Poetry from Appalachia*, edited by Jeff Mann and Julia Watts, 58. Morgantown: West Virginia University Press, 2019.
Davenport, Guy. "Appalachian Gothic: Review of *Outer Dark* by Cormac McCarthy." *The New York Times*, September 29, 1968. https://www.nytimes.com/1968/09/29/archives/appalachian-gothic.html.
Davis, Rebecca Harding. "Life in the Iron Mills." In *The Norton Anthology of American Literature: 1820-1865*, edited by Robert S. Levine and Arnold Krupat, 2599–2625. New York: W.W. Norton and Company, 2007. First published 1861 by The Atlantic Monthly (Washington-, DC).
———. "David Gaunt." In *Rebecca Harding Davis's Stories of the Civil War: Selected Writings form the Borderlands*, edited by Sharon M. Harris and Robin L. Cadwallader. Athens: University of Georgia Press, 2010. Kindle. First published 1862 by The Atlantic Monthly (Washington, DC).
Davison, Carol Margaret. "The Gothic and Addiction: A Mad Tango." *Gothic Studies* 11, no. 2 (November 2009): 1–8. https://doi.org/10.7227/GS.11.2.2.
———. Introduction – The Corpse in the Closet: The Gothic, Death, and Modernity to *The Gothic and Death*, edited by Carol Margaret Davison, 1–17. Manchester: Manchester University Press, 2017.
Deckard, Sharae. "'Uncanny States': Global Eco-gothic and the World Ecology in Rana Dasgupta's Tokyo Cancelled." In *Ecogothic*, edited by Andrew Smith and William Hughes, 177–194. Manchester: Manchester University Press, 2013.
Deer Cloud, Susan. "Mountaintops, Appalachia." In *Mountains Piled upon Mountains*, edited by Jessica Corey, 104–106. Morgantown: West Virginia University Press, 2019.
Dickey, James. *Deliverance*. Boston: Houghton Mifflin, 1970.
Douglass, Tom. Foreword, Hawk's Nest: A Novel's of America's Disinherited to *Hawk's Nest*, edited by Hubert Skidmore, vii–xvii. Knoxville: University of Tennessee Press, 2004.
Duck, Leigh Anne. "Undead Genres/Living Locales: Gothic Legacies in *The True Meaning of Pictures* and *Winter's Bone*." In *Undead Souths: The Gothic and Beyond in Southern Literature and Culture*, edited by Eric Gary Anderson, Taylor Hagood, and Daniel Cross Turner, 173–186. Baton Rouge: Louisiana State University Press, 2015.
Dunn, Steven. *Potted Meat*. Grafton: Tarpaulin Sky Press, 2016.
———. *Water & Power*. Grafton: Tarpaulin Sky Press, 2018.
Dutton, Justin Ray. "Challenging Dominant Christianity's Queerphobic Rhetoric." In *Storytelling in Queer Appalachia: Imagining and Writing the Unspeakable Other*, edited by Hillery Glasby, Sherrie Gradin, and Rachael Ryerson, 37–57. Morgantown: West Virginia University Press, 2020.
Dykeman, Wilma. *Return the Innocent Earth*. New York: Holt,: Rhinehart and Winston, 1973.
Edwards, Justin D., Rune Graulund and Johan Höglund. Introduction: Gothic in the Anthropocene to *Dark Scenes from Damaged Earth: The Gothic Anthropocene*, edited by Justin D. Edwards, Rune Graulund, and Johan Höglund, ix–xxvi. Minneapolis: University of Minnesota Press, 2022.

Efstathiou Jr., Jim and Mark Drajem. "Fracking Companies Silence Water Complaints with Sealed Settlements." *Insurance Journal*, June 10, 2013. https://www.insurancejournal.com/news/national/2013/06/10/294608.htm.

Eller, Ronald D. Foreword to *Back Talk from Appalachia: Confronting Stereotypes*, edited by Dwight B. Billings, Gurney Norman, and Katherine Ledford, ix–xi. Lexington: The University Press of Kentucky, 1999.

EPA: United States Environmental Protection Agency. "Hydraulic Fracturing for Oil and Gas: Impacts from the Hydraulic Fracturing Water Cycle on Drinking Water Resources in the United States (Final Report)." Accessed January 17, 2023. https://cfpub.epa.gov/ncea/hfstudy/recordisplay.cfm?deid=332990.

Estok, Simon C. "Theorizing in a Space of Ambivalent Openness: Ecocriticism and Ecophobia." *Interdisciplinary Studies in Literature and the Environment* 16, no. 2 (Spring 2009): 203–225. https://www.jstor.org/stable/44733418.

Evans, Jedidiah. *Look Abroad, Angel: Thomas Wolfe and the Geographies of Longing*. Athens: University of Georgia Press, 2020.

Fauth, RK. *A Dream In Which I Am Playing With Bees*. Lubbock: Texas Tech University Press, 2024.

Feldman, Chanda. *Approaching the Fields: Poems*. Baton Rouge: Louisiana State University Press, 2018.

Fox, John Jr. *The Trail of the Lonesome Pine*. New York, 1912; *Project Gutenberg*, December 21, 2023. https://www.gutenberg.org/files/5122/5122-h/5122-h.htm.

Franks, Julia. *The Say So*. Spartanburg: Hub City Press, 2023.

Friedman, Gabriella. "Illegible Histories, Invisible Movements: Indigenous Refusal in Blake Hausman's *Riding the Trail of Tears*." *PMLA* 138, no. 1 (2023): 83–97. https://doi.org/10.1632/S0030812922000979.

Gaffney, Austyn. "A Small Town's Battle Against Radioactive Fracking Waste." *NDRC*, January 9, 2019. https://www.nrdc.org/stories/small-towns-battle-against-radioactive-fracking-waste.

Gainer, Patrick W. *Witches, Ghosts and Signs: Folklore of the Southern Appalachians*. Morgantown: West Virginia University Press, 2008.

Gatlin, Jill. "Disturbing Aesthetics: Industrial Pollution, Moral Discourse, and Narrative Form in Rebecca Harding Davis's 'Life in the Iron Mills'." *Nineteenth-century Literature* 68, no. 2 (2013): 201–233. https://www.jstor.org/stable/10.1525/ncl.2013.68.2.201

Giardina, Denise. *The Unquiet Earth*. New York: Ivy Books, 1992.

———. "Appalachian Images: A Personal History." In *Back Talk from Appalachia: Confronting Stereotypes*, edited by Dwight B. Billings, Gurney Norman and Katherine Ledford, 161–173. Lexington: The University Press of Kentucky, 1999.

Giovanni, Nikki. *The Collected Poetry of Nikki Giovanni: 1968-1998*. New York: HarperCollins e-books, 2008. Kindle.

———. *Make Me Rain: Poems and Prose*. New York: William Morrow, 2020.

Glasby, Hillery, Sherrie Gradin and Rachael Ryerson. Introduction to *Storytelling in Queer Appalachia: Imagining and Writing the Unspeakable Other*, edited by Hillery Glasby, Sherrie Gradin, and Rachael Ryerson, 1–15. Morgantown: West Virginia University Press, 2020.

Goddu, Teresa A. *Gothic America: Narrative, History, and Nation*. New York: Columbia University Press, 1997.

Goff, Lorelei. "Cougar: Ghost of Appalachia." *Appalachian Voice*, February 17, 2016. https://appvoices.org/2016/02/17/cougar/.

WORKS CITED

Good, Crystal. *Valley Girl*. Self-published, Amazon, 2012.
Gordon, Avery. *Ghostly Matters: Haunting and the Sociological Imagination*. Minneapolis: University of Minnesota Press, 2008. First published 1997 by University of Minnesota Press (Minneapolis).
Graves, Jesse. *Basin Ghosts*. Huntsville: Texas Review Press, 2014.
Graves, Jesse and William Wright. *Specter Mountain: Poems*. Macon: Mercer University Press, 2018.
Greene, Amy. *Long Man*. New York: Alfred A Knopf, 2014.
Haigh, Jennifer. *Heat and Light*. New York: HarperCollins, 2017. First published 2016 by HarperCollins (New York).
Haldorson, Sally. "Frankenstein and an Empire of Pain." *Porchlight*, May 7, 2021. https://www.porchlightbooks.com/blog/managing-directors-cut/frankenstein-and-an-empire-of-pain.
Hampton, Leah. *Fuckface and Other Stories*. New York: Henry Holt, 2020.
Harvey, Chelsea. "'We are Climate Zero.' Why Appalachia Faces Perilous Floods." *Climate Wire*, March 8, 2022. https://www.eenews.net/articles/we-are-climate-zero-why-appalachia-faces-perilous-floods/.
Hausman, Blake M. *Riding the Trail of Tears*. Lincoln: University of Nebraska Press, 2011.
Heart of Appalachia. "Trail of the Lonesome Pine: Outdoor Drama." Accessed December 28, 2023. https://heartofappalachia.com/event/trail-of-the-lonesome-pine-outdoor-drama/var/ri-15.l-L1/#:~:text=In%202023%2C%20the%20Trail%20of,beginning%20nightly%20at%208%20p.m.
Henry, Matthew S. "Extractive Fictions and Postextraction Futurisms: Energy and Environmental Injustice in Appalachia." *Environmental Humanities* 11, no. 2 (November 2019): 402–426. https://doi.org/10.1215/22011919-7754534.
———. *Hydronarratives: Water, Environmental Justice, and a Just Transition*. Lincoln: University of Nebraska Press, 2022.
Hill, Elaine L. and Lala Ma. "Drinking Water, Fracking, and Infant Health." *Journal of Health Economics* 82 (2022): 1–18. https://doi.org/10.1016/j.jhealeco.2022.102595.
Hill, Halle. *Good Women*. Spartenberg: Hub City Press, 2023.
Hock, Stephen. Introduction to *Trump Fiction: Essays on Donald Trump in Literature, Film and Television*, edited by Stephen Hock, 1–17. Lanham: Lexington Books, 2020.
Höglund, Johan. *The American Imperial Gothic: Popular Culture, Empire, Violence*. London: Routledge, 2014.
hooks, bell. *Talking Back: Thinking Feminist, Thinking Black*. New York: Routledge, 2015.
———. *Appalachian Elegy: Poetry and Place*. Lexington: University Press of Kentucky, 2012. Copyright © 2012 Gloria Jean Watkins (bell hooks). Reprinted by permission of The University Press of Kentucky.
House, Silas. "A Conscious Heart." *Journal of Appalachian Studies* 14, no. 1–2 (Spring-Fall 2008): 7–19. https://www.jstor.org/stable/41446798.
———. *Southernmost*. Chapel Hill: Algonquin Books, 2018.
Inscoe, John C. and Gordon B. McKinney. *The Heart of Confederate Appalachia: Western North Carolina in the Civil War*. Chapel Hill: University of North Carolina Press, 2000.
IPPC: The Intergovernmental Panel on Climate Change. "Global Warming of 1.5°C: Special Report: FAQ Chapter 1." Accessed December 28, 2023. https://www.ipcc.ch/sr15/faq/faq-chapter-1/#:~:text=Human%2Dinduced%20warming%20reached%20approximately,emissions%20reaching%20zero%20by%202055.

Jerolmack, Colin. "The Fracking Boom is over. Where did All the Jobs Go?" *MIT Technology Review*, July 1, 2021. https://www.technologyreview.com/2021/07/01/1027822/fracking-boom-jobs-industry/.

Johnson, Fenton. *Scissors, Paper, Rock*. New York: Pocket Books, 1993.

Jones III, Oliver King. "Social Criticism in the Works of Wilma Dykeman." In *American Vein: Critical Readings in Appalachian Literature*, edited by Danny L. Miller, Sharon Hatfield, and Gurney Norman, 73–90. Athens: Ohio University Press, 2005.

Joy, David. *The Weight of this World*. New York: G.P. Putnam's Sons, 2017.

———. *Where All Light Tends To Go*. New York: G.P. Putnam's Sons, 2020. First published 2015 by G.P Putnam's Sons (New York).

———. *When These Mountains Burn*. London: Andre Deutsch, 2020.

———. *Those We Thought We Knew*. New York: G.P. Putnam's Sons, 2023.

Kaufmann, Alexander. "The Lithium War Next Door." *HuffPost*. May 22, 2022. https://www.huffingtonpost.co.uk/entry/piedmont-lithium-mine_n_62869f4be4b0933e7362d58c.Keefe, Patrick Radden. *Empire of Pain*. New York: Doubleday, 2021.

Kingsolver, Barbara. *Demon Copperhead*. London: Faber and Faber, 2022.

Klein, Naomi. *This Changes Everything: Capitalism vs. the Climate*. New York: Penguin, 2015. First published 2014 by Simon and Shuster (New York).

Klesta, Matt. "Resilience and Recovery: Insights from the 2022 Eastern Kentucky Flood." *Federal Reserve Bank of Cleveland*. https://doi.org/10.26509/frbc-cd-20230927.

Kwong, Lisa. *Becoming Appalasian*. Glenview: Glass Lyre Press, 2022.

Ledford, Katherine. "A Landscape and a People Set Apart: Narratives of Exploration and Travel in Early Appalachia." In *Back Talk from Appalachia: Confronting Stereotypes*, edited by Dwight B. Billings, Gurney Norman, and Katherine Ledford, 47–66. Lexington: The University Press of Kentucky, 1999.

Linneman, Travis and Corina Medley. "Down and Out in Middleton and Jackson: Drugs, Dependency, and Decline in J.D. Vance's Capitalist Realism." In *Appalachian Reckoning: A Region Responds to Hillbilly Elegy*, edited by Anthony Harkins and Meredith McCarroll, 136–154. Morgantown: West Virginia University Press, 2019.

Locklear, Erica Abrams. "Not Either/Or, But Both: Cherokee and Appalachian Identity in Annette Saunooke Clapsaddle's *Even As We Breathe*." *North Carolina Literary Review* 32 (2023): 26–39. https://www.proquest.com/scholarly-journals/not-either-both-cherokee-appalachian-identity/docview/2837141707/se-2.

Lucas, Megan. *Here in the Dark*. Charleston: Shotgun Honey, 2023.

Maimon, Alan. *Twilight in Hazard: An Appalachian Reckoning*. Brooklyn: Melville House, 2021.

Maren, Mesha. *Sugar Run*. 2018. Chapel Hill: Algonquin Books, 2019.

———. *Perpetual West*. Chapel Hill: Algonquin Books, 2022.

Marsh, Whitney, Heith Copes, and Travis Linnemann. "Creating Visual Differences: Methamphetamine Users Perceptions of Anti-meth Campaigns." *International Journal of Drug Policy* 23 (2017): 52–61. https://doi-org.ezproxy.uwe.ac.uk/10.1016/j.drugpo.2016.09.001.

Massie, Elizabeth. *Sineater*. Hertford: Crossroad Press, 2013. First published 1992 by Carroll and Graf (New York).

———. *Desper Hollow*. Hertford: Crossroad Press, 2023. First published 2013 by Apex Publishing (Lexington).

Mathews, Daniel. *Trees in Trouble: Wildfires, Infestations, and Climate Change*. Berkeley: Counterpoint, 2021. First published 2020 by Counterpoint (Berkeley).

McCarthy, Cormac. *Child of God*. London: Picador, 1989. First published 1973 by Random House (New York).

McClanahan, Bill. "Earth-world-planet: Rural Ecologies of Horror and Dark Green Criminology." *Theoretical Criminology* 24, no. 4 (2020): 633–650. https://doi.org/10.1177/1362480618819813.

McCollum, Victoria. Introduction to *Make America Hate Again*, edited by Victoria McCollum, 1–15. New York: Routledge 2020.

McCrumb, Sharyn. *Ghost Riders*. New York: Dutton, 2003.

McKinney, George B. "The Civil War and Reconstruction." In *High Mountains Rising: Appalachia in Time and Place*, edited by Richard A. Straw and H. Tyler Blethen, 46–58. Urbana: University of Illinois Press, 2004.

McLarney, Rose. *Its Day Being Gone*. New York: Penguin, 2014.

McLennon, Leigh M. "'The Red Thirst is on this Nation': Vampiric Hauntings and the American Civil War." In *War Gothic in Literature and Culture*, edited by Agnieszka Soltysik Monnet and Steffen Hantke, 2–21. New York: Routledge, 2016.

McNally, David. *Monsters of the Market: Zombies, Vampires and Global Capitalism*. Chicago: Haymarket Books, 2012. First published 2011 by Brill (Leiden).

McNeil, Zane. Introduction to *Y'all Means All: The Emerging Voices Queering Appalachia*, edited by Z. Zane Mitchell, 1–12. Oakland: PM Press, 2022.

McNeill, Louise. *Gauley Mountain: A History in Verse*. New York: Harcourt Brace, 1996. First published 1939 by McClain (West Virginia).

Mehta, Rahul. *No Other World*. New York; Harper Perennial, 2017.

———. *Feeding the Ghosts: Poems*. Lexington: The University Press of Kentucky, 2024.

Meit, Michael, Megan Heffernan, and Erin Tanenbaum. "Investigating the Impact of Diseases of Despair in Appalachia." *Journal of Appalachian Health* 1, no. 2 (2019): 7–18. https://doi.org/10.13023/jah.0102.02.

Miller, Danny L., Sharon Hatfield, and Gurney Norman. *American Vein: Critical Readings in Appalachian* Literature. Athens: Ohio University Press, 2005.

Miller, Elizabeth Carolyn. *Extraction Ecologies and the Literature of the Long Exhaustion*. Princeton: Princeton University Press, 2021.

Molesky, Jason. "Gothic Toxicity and the Mysteries of Nondisclosure in American Hydrofracking Literature." *Modern Fiction Studies* 66, no. 1 (Spring 2020): 52–77. https://doi.org/10.1353/mfs.2020.0002.

Monnet, Agnieszka Soltysik. "Gothic Matters: Introduction." *Text Matters* 6, no. 6 (2016): 7–14. https://doi.org/10.1515/texmat-2016-0001.https://journals.openedition.org/jsse/3122.

Monnet, Agnieszka Soltysik and Steffen Hantke. "Ghosts from the Battlefields: A Short Historical Introduction to the War Gothic." In *War Gothic in Literature and Culture*, edited by Agnieszka Soltysik Monnet and Steffen Hantke, xi–xxv. New York: Routledge, 2016.

Mooney, Steve. "Agrarian Tragedy: Harriet Arnow's *The Dollmaker*." *Appalachian Journal* 19, no. 1 (Fall 1991): 34–42. https://www.jstor.org/stable/40933316.

Moreau, Julia. "How will Roe v. Wade Reversal Affect LGBTQ Rights? Experts, Advocates Weigh in." *NBC News*, June 24, 2022. https://www.nbcnews.com/nbc-out/out-news/will-roe-v-wade-reversal-affect-lgbtq-rights-experts-advocates-weigh-rcna35284.

Nash, Susan Smith. "Fracking Novels: Scrabble, Zombies, and the Problematized Real." *World Literature Today* 91, no. 2 (April 2017): 60–63. https://doi.org/10.7588/worllitetoda.91.2.0060.

Noe, Kenneth W. "'Deadened Color and Colder Horror': Rebecca Harding Davis and the Myth of Unionist Appalachia." In *Back Talk from Appalachia: Confronting Stereotypes*, edited by Dwight B. Billings, Gurney Norman, and Katherine Ledford, 67–84. Lexington: University Press of Kentucky, 1999.

Norman, Gurney. *Kinfolks: The Wilgus Stories*. New York: Avon Printing, 1986. First published 1977 by Gnomon Press (Frankfort).

Null, Matthew Neill. *Allegheny Front*. Louisville: Sarabande Books, 2016.

Offutt, Chris. *The Killing Hills*. New York: Grove Press, 2021.

———. *Shifty's Boys*. Harpenden: No Exit Press, 2022.

———. *Code of the Hills*. New York: Grove Press, 2023.

Olsen, Ted. "Literature." In *High Mountains Rising: Appalachia in Time and Place*, edited by Richard A. Straw and H. Tyler Blethen, 165–178. Urbana: University of Illinois Press, 2004.

Otjen, Nathaniel. "When Things Hail: The Material Encounter in Anthropocene Literature." *Configurations* 28, no. 3 (Summer 2002): 285–307. https://doi.org/10.1353/con.2020.0018.

Owen, Sheldon. "Living with Black Bears in West Virginia." *Extension*, January 2021. https://extension.wvu.edu/natural-resources/wildlife/black-bears#:~:text=By%20the%20early%201970s%2C%20the,bright%20for%20the%20black%20bear.

Page, Myra. *Daughter of the Hills: A Woman's Part in the Coal Miners' Struggle*. New York: The Feminist Press, 1977. First published 1950 by The Citadel Press (New York).

Palmer, Paulina. *The Queer Uncanny: New Perspectives on the Gothic*. Cardiff: University of Wales Press, 2012.

Pancake, Ann. *Given Ground*. Hanover: University Press of New England, 2001.

———. *Strange As This Weather Has Been*. Berkeley: Counterpoint, 2007.

———. "Letter to West Virginia, November 2016." In *Mountains Piled Upon Mountains: Appalachian Nature Writing in the Anthropocene*, edited by Jessica Carey, 239–242. Morgantown: West Virginia University Press, 2019.

Pancake, Breece D.J. *The Stories of Breece D'J Pancake*. Boston: Back Bay Books, 2002. First published 1983 by Little Brown (Boston).

Panowich, Brian. *Bull Mountain*. New York: G. P. Putnam's Sons, 2015.

———. *Like Lions*. London: Head of Zeus, 2018.

Parker, Elizabeth. *The Forest and the EcoGothic: The Deep Dark Woods in the Popular Imagination*. London: Palgrave Macmillan, 2020.

Perdue, Theda. "Red and Black in the Southern Appalachians." In *Blacks in Appalachia*, edited by William H. Turner and Edward J. Cabbell, 23–29. Lexington: The University Press of Kentucky, 1985.

Powell, Mark. *The Dark Corner*. Knoxville: University of Tennessee Press, 2012.

———. *The Sheltering*. Columbia: University of South Carolina Press, 2014.

———. *Small Treasons*. New York: Gallery Books, 2017.

———. *Lioness*. Morgantown: West Virginia University Press, 2022.

———. *The Late Rebellion*. Raleigh: Regal House Publishing, 2024.

Presley, Erin M. "Reconciling Literacy and Loss in Ron Rash's *Nothing Gold Can Stay*." *Journal of the Short Story in English* 74 (Spring 2020): 189–200. https://journals.openedition.org/jsse/3122.

Rash, Ron. *Raising the Dead*. Oak Ridge: Iris Press, 2002.

———. *Nothing Gold Can Stay*. New York: HarperCollins, 2003.

———. *The World Made Straight*. New York: Picador, 2007.

———. "Shelton Laurel." *Ploughshares* 34, no. 1 (Spring 2008): 145. https://www.jstor.org/stable/40354301.

———. *Burning Bright*. New York: Ecco/HarperCollins, 2010.

Redding, Arthur F. *Haints: American Ghosts, Millennial Passions, and Contemporary Gothic Fictions*. Tuscaloosa: The University of Alabama Press, 2011.

Regal House Publishing. "Mark Powell." Accessed December 28, 2023. https://regalhousepublishing.com/mark-powell/.

Reilly, Matthew J. et al. "Drivers and Ecological Impacts of a Wildfire Outbreak in the Southern Appalachian Mountains after Decades of Fire Exclusion." *Forest Ecology and Management* 524 (2022): 1–12. https://doi.org/10.1016/j.foreco.2022.120500.

Reuters, "Global Demand for Lithium Batteries to Leap Five-Fold by 2023 – Li Bridge." February 15, 2023. https://www.reuters.com/markets/commodities/global-demand-lithium-batteries-leap-five-fold-by-2030-li-bridge-2023-02-15/.

Roberson, Ed. *Asked What Has Changed*. Middletown: Wesleyan University Press, 2021.

Robertson, Sarah. "Gothic Appalachian Literature." In *The Palgrave Handbook of the Southern Gothic*, edited by Susan Castillo and Charles Crow, 109–120. London: Palgrave Macmillan, 2016.

Robinson, Richard Knox. "From The Kallikaks to The Kallikaks: *Hillbilly Elegy* and the Legacy of Eugenics." *Film Criticism* 46, no. 2 (2022): 1–27. https://journals.publishing.umich.edu/fc/article/id/3610/.

Satterwhite, Emily. *Dear Appalachia: Readers, Identity, and Popular Fiction since 1878*. Lexington: University Press of Kentucky, 2011.

Saunooke Clapsaddle, Annette. *Even As We Breathe*. Lexington: Fireside Industries Books, 2020.

Scanlan, Stephen J. "'Mined' for Its Citizens? Poverty, Opportunity Structure, and Appalachian Soldier Deaths in the Iraq War." *Journal of Appalachian Studies* 20, no. 1 (Spring 2014): 43–67. https://doi.org/10.5406/jappastud.20.1.0043.

Schenkkan, Robert. *The Kentucky Cycle*. New York: Dramatists Play Service, Inc, 1993.

Scott, Rebecca R. *Removing Mountains: Extracting Nature and Identity in the Appalachian Coalfields*. Minneapolis: University of Minnesota Press, 2010.

Sickels, Carter. *The Prettiest Star*. Spartanburg: Hub City Press, 2020.

Sipple, Savannah. *WWJD and other poems*. Little Rock: Sibling Rivalry Press, 2019.

Skidmore, Hubert. *Hawk's Nest*. New York, 1941; Knoxville: University of Tennessee Press, 2004. First published 1941 by Doubleday, Doran (New York).

Smith, Andrew. *Gothic Literature*. 2nd ed. Edinburgh: Edinburgh University Press, 2013.

Smith, Andrew and William Hughes. Introduction: Defining the Eco-gothic to *Ecogothic*, edited by Andrew Smith and William Hughes, 1–14. Manchester: Manchester University Press, 2013.

Smith, Barbara Ellen. "De-gradations of Whiteness: Appalachia and the Complexities of Race." *Journal of Appalachian Studies* 10, no. 1/2 (April 2004): 38–57. http://www.jstor.org/stable/41446605.

Somerville, Siobhan B. Introduction to *The Cambridge Companion to Queer Studies*, edited by Siobhan B. Somerville, 1–13. Cambridge: Cambridge University Press, 2020.

Spoth, Daniel. *Ruin and Resilience: Southern Literature and the Environment*. Baton Rouge: Louisiana State University Press, 2023.

Stark, Hannah, Katrina Schlunke and Penny Edmonds. "Introduction: Uncanny Objects in the Anthropocene." *Australian Humanities Review* 63 (November 2018):

22–27. https://www.proquest.com/scholarly-journals/introduction-uncanny-objects-anthropocene/docview/2160345660/se-2.

Straw, Richard A. Introduction to *High Mountains Rising: Appalachia in Time and Place*, edited by Richard A. Straw and H. Tyler Blethen, 1–6. Urbana: University of Illinois Press, 2004.

Thorpe, Charles. *Necroculture*. New York: Palgrave Macmillan, 2016.

Truscello, Michael. *Infrastructural Brutalism: Art and the Necropolitics of Infrastructure*. Cambridge, MA: The MIT Press, 2020.

Tsing, Anna Lowenhaupt, et al. Introduction: Haunted Landscapes of the Anthropocene to *Arts of Living on a Damaged Planet: Ghosts and Monsters of the Anthropocene*, edited by Anna Lowenhaupt Tsing, Heather Anne Swanson, Elaine Gan and Nils Bubant, 1–14. Minneapolis: University of Minnesota Press, 2017.

Turner, Daniel Cross. "Gray Ghosts: Remediating the Confederate Undead." In *Undead Souths: The Gothic and Beyond in Southern Literature and Culture*, edited by Eric Gary Anderson, Taylor Hagood, and Daniel Cross Turner, 52–63. Baton Rouge: Louisiana State University Press, 2015.

Turner, William H. Introduction to *Blacks in Appalachia*, edited by William H. Turner and Edward J. Cabbell, xvii–xxiii. Lexington: The University Press of Kentucky, 1985.

———.. *The Harlan Renaissance: Stories of Black Life in Appalachian Coal Towns*. Morgantown: West Virginia University Press, 2021.

Unrue, Darlene H. "The Gothic Matrix of *Look Homeward, Angel*." In *Critical Essays on Thomas Wolfe*, edited by John S. Phillipson, 48–56. Boston: G.K Hall & Co, 1985.

Vance, J.D. *Hillbilly Elegy: A Memoir of a Family in Crisis*. London: William Collins, 2016.

Walker, Frank X. *Affrilachia*. Lexington: Old Cove Press, 2000.

———. *About Flight*. Lexington: Accents Publishing, 2015.

———. *Masked Man, Black: Pandemic and Protest Poems*. Lexington: Accents Publishing, 2020.

Waller Smith, Effie. *The Collected Works of Effie Waller Smith*. New York: Oxford University Press, 1991.

Walters, Joanna. "Kamala Harris Warns of Threats to LGBTQ+ Rights during Visit to Stonewall." *The Guardian*, June 27, 2023. https://www.theguardian.com/us-news/2023/jun/26/kamala-harris-stonewall-inn-visit-pride-month.

Watts, Julia. *Lovesick Blossoms*. New York: Three Rooms Press, 2023.

———. "Author Interview: Julia Watts." By Kat Georges. *Three Rooms Press*, September 30, 2023. https://threeroomspress.com/2023/09/author-interview-julia-watts/.

Wellman, Manly Wade. *John the Balladeer*. Richmond: Valancourt Books, 2023. First published 1988 by Baen Books (Riverdale).

Westengard, Laura. *Gothic Queer Culture: Marginalized Communities and the Ghosts of Insidious Trauma*. Lincoln: University of Nebraska Press, 2019.

Wester, Maisha L. *African American Gothic: Screams from Shadowed Places*. New York: Palgrave Macmillan, 2012.

White, Charles Dodd. *How Fire Runs*. Athens, Ohio: Swallow Press, 2020.

Wilber, Tom. *Under the Surface: Fracking, Fortunes, and the Fate of the Marcellus Shale*. New York: Cornell University Press, 2012.

Wills, Matthew. "Remembering the Disaster at Hawks Nest." *JSTOR Daily*, October 30, 2020. https://daily.jstor.org/remembering-the-disaster-at-hawks-nest/.

Wilson, Darlene. "A Judicious Combination of Incident and Psychology: John Fox Jr. and the Southern Mountaineer Motif." In *Back Talk from Appalachia: Confronting Stereotypes*, edited by Dwight B. Billings, Gurney Norman, and Katherine Ledford, 98–118. Lexington: The University Press of Kentucky, 1999.

Wolfe, Thomas. *Look Homeward, Angel*. London: Penguin, 2016. First published 1929 by Charles Scribner's Sons (New York).

Index

1959 Knox Mine Disaster 31

About Flight (Walker) 29
Affrilachia 57; movement 11
Alice in Wonderland 47
Allison, Dorothy 62
Althofer, Jayson 28
American Civil Liberties Union 63
American eugenics movement 1
American imperial gothic 18, 23
Anderson, Eric Gary 54
Another Appalachia (Avashia) 62
Anthropocene 41–42, 48–49, 71, 73; anthropogenic harm 36
Appalachian basin 38
Appalachian Christian queerphobic rhetoric (ACQR) 65
Appalachian culture 3, 53; Appalachian superstitions 1–2
Appalachian Elegy (hooks) 21, 36, 61
Appalachian folklore 1, 3, 13n5; storytelling 1, 48, 54, 57, 59–60
Appalachian gothic pharmography 19, 29
Appalachian noir: Chris Offutt 26–27, 40–41; David Joy 12, 25, 42–43, 59–60; Ron Rash 20, 22, 27–29
Appalachian Regional Commission (ARC) 3
Appalachian Studies Association conference 36
Arlington National Cemetery 23
Arnow, Harriette 9–10
Asked What Has Changed (Roberson) 42
Attaway, William 10
Avashia, Neema 62

Bakken formation 2
Bathanti, Joseph 36
Batteau, Allen 2–3

benzodiazepine 25
Big Pharma 17, 25, 30
Big Stone Gap, Virginia 7
Billings, Dwight B. 3–4, 13n25, 19
"Bitch Baby" (Hill) 66
Black Appalachians 11, 54; Affrilachia 11, 24, 36, 57, 60; Lost Cause 18; slavery 3, 53, 57–58, 71
Black Arts Movement 11
Black-on-Black violence 57–58
Blacks in Appalachia 54
Blethen, H. Tyler 54
Blood on the Forge (Attaway) 10
Blue Ridge Landfill 40
bodies 7, 12, 20, 23, 25, 27, 63–64; body dysmorphia 65
"Boom Boom" (Good) 36
"Boomer" (Hampton) 44
Botting, Fred 2, 6, 71
Braudy, Leo 26
Brinkmeyer, Robert 28
Brown, Karida L. 8
Brown, Taylor 1
Buffalo Creek disaster 37
Bureau of Investigative Journalism, The 22
Burnham, Michelle 56
"But We Lived" (Feldman) 2
Butler, Tom 30

Cabbell, Edward J. 54
Canadian Tar Sands 2
capitalism 2, 7–8, 10, 26, 28, 30, 35–36, 39, 71; capitalist grotesque 8; capitalist wage-labor system 10; industry 41; late capitalism 39; neoliberalism 28, 39
Carey, Allison 61
"Cascade" (Roberson) 58
Castro, Joy 5

Catte, Elizabeth 43
Child of God (McCarthy) 12
Civil War 17–22, 25; guerilla war tactics 20; monuments 60
Claborn, John 10
climate crisis: Anthropocene 41–42, 48–49, 71, 73; biosphere 25, 49; climate activism 38, 48; climate change 41, 43–45; ecoterrorism 47–49; environment 2–3, 7–8, 19, 35–41, 45–48, 61, 71; flooding 37, 41–42; green transition 71–72; sixth mass extinction 41, 45–49; wildfires 5, 41–45, 49
Clines, Francis X 37
Cloud, Susan Deer 36
Code of the Hills, The (Offutt) 27
collateral damage 8, 22, 24, 30
"Commander-in-Cheat" (Walker) 72
contemporary gothic 4–5, 11–12, 19, 23, 25, 30, 41, 43, 47, 49, 72–73
Cooper, Lydia 11
Corcoran, Jonathan 62
Crane, David 47
creatures 1–3, 43, 67
Croley, Michael 37, 59
Crowe, Thomas Rain 55

Dark Corner, The (Powell) 23–24
dark ecology 46, 71
Daughter of the Hills (Page) 8
Davenport, doris 57, 64
Davenport, Guy 1
David Copperfield (Dickens) 29
Davis, Rebecca Harding 6–7, 18
Davison, Carol 17, 26, 28
death 8, 18–20, 23–26, 28–29, 47–48, 55–56, 58, 60; gothic pharmography 17, 19, 29; life expectancy 26; suicide 19, 21, 23–25
Deckard, Sharae 71
Deliverance (Dickey) 1
Demon Copperhead (Kingsolver) 29–31
demons 5, 25, 31, 43
Department for Defense 25
Devil's Oven (Benedict) 12
Dickens, Charles 29
Dickey, James 1
diseases of despair: addiction 17, 19, 25, 28–31, 43; alcohol 19, 24; big pharma 17, 25, 30; drugs 27; heroin 25, 27; meth 5, 25, 27–28; methamphetamine users 19; opioids 27, 29–30; recovery 29–31

Dobbs v. Jackson 72
Dollmaker, The (Arnow) 9–10
Douglass, Tom 8
Dream in Which I Am Playing With Bees, A (Fauth) 45–46
"Drought Year" (Graves) 41
Duck, Leigh Anne 4
Dunn, Steven 22–23, 25
Dutton, Justin Ray 65
Dykeman, Wilma 10–11

Eastern Band of Cherokee Indians (EBCI) 54–57
eco-terrorism 47–49
Eller, Ronald 1, 3
Evans, Jedidiah 9
Even As We Breathe (Saunooke Clapsaddle) 54, 56–57
extraction: deforestation 8, 11, 26, 35, 42; extractive fictions 36–41; extractive industries 2, 26, 30, 49; infrastructural brutalism 8, 39; lithium 71; sacrifice zone 2, 7, 72; slurry spills 36–38; *see also* fossil fuels
extractive logic 2–3, 7–8, 35–36, 38, 41, 61, 71–72

farming 9–10, 25, 38
far-right extremism 5, 43–44, 53, 60, 66
Faulkner, William 9
Fauth, R. K. 46
Feeding the Ghosts (Mehta) 62–63
Feldman, Chanda 2
Finney, Nikky 11, 24–25, 45
Flight Risk (Castro) 5
fossil fuels: coal 2, 7, 10, 17, 19, 30, 35–38, 49, 71–72; extraction 2–4, 35–42, 49, 71–72; fracking 35–36, 38–40; fracking boom 38, 40; fracking towers 38–39; fracking waste 40–41; hydrofracking literature 38; mountain top removal 30, 35–38, 42, 72; strip mining 11, 36–37, 46
Fox, John 7
fracking: *see* fossil fuels
Frankenstein (Shelley) 26, 67
Franks, Julia 72
Fraser, Max 9

Gauley Mountain: A History in Verse (McNeill) 8
Gay, William 12
geopolitics 23–24

INDEX

Ghost Riders (Sharyn) 20
"Ghostless" (Pancake) 20
ghosts 1, 7–9, 13n5, 17, 20–24, 27, 29, 36, 45, 48, 55, 57, 61; haunted house 27–28; haunting 1, 8–9, 20–28, 31, 36–38, 40, 45–46, 48, 53–59, 61
Giardina, Denise 36–38
Giovanni, Nikki 24, 72
Goddu, Teresa 3, 53
Gods of Howl Mountain (Brown) 1
Good, Crystal 11, 36
Gordon, Avery 40
gothic pharmography 17, 19, 29
gothic tropes 2–3, 7, 11, 25, 31, 38–40, 43, 49, 60, 62, 64, 73; gothic frisson 42
graves 12, 20–21, 32n29, 48, 56, 59, 61; graveyard 11
Graves, Jesse 25, 41
Great Migration 9
grotesque 7–8, 11–12, 24

Haigh, Jennifer 38–40
"Halloween 2017" (Davenport) 64
Hampton, Leah 44
Hantke, Steffan 17–18
Harvey, Chelsea 41
Hausman, Blake M. 54
Hawks Nest (Skidmore) 8
Hawks Nest Disaster 8
Heat and Light (Haigh) 38–40
Heffernan, Megan 26
Henry, Matthew S. 36–37, 67
Hill, Elaine L. 39
Hill, Halle 66
hillbillies 1, 6, 27
Hillbilly Elegy 1, 25, 30–31
Höglund, Johan 18, 23
hooks, bell 11, 21, 36, 60–61
horror 2–5, 7, 9, 12, 18–19, 21–23, 25–31, 35–38, 40–42, 47–49, 54–55, 57, 60, 65–66, 71–72
House, Silas 36, 65
How Fire Runs (White) 43–44
Hughes, William 43
hydrofracking fiction 38

immigration 1, 58, 73
Indigenous Appalachians: Cherokee 6, 54–55, 57, 59; Chickasaws 54; Choctaw 6, 54; Creeks 54; EBCI 54–57; genocide and removal 21, 25, 54–55, 71; Shawnees 54; storytelling 54
infrastructural brutalism 8, 39

Inscoe, John C. 20
intersectionality 5, 11, 53, 56–57, 61
Iraq War 18, 22–25
Islamophobia 53

Johnson, Fenton 62
Johnson, LaVena 24–25, 33n62
Jones, Oliver 11
Joy, David 12, 22, 25–27, 41–43, 59–60

Kentucky Cycle, The (Schenkkan) 1
Killing Hills, The (Offutt) 26–27
Kingsolver, Barbara 29–31
"Kittens" (Lucas) 29
Klein, Naomi 2
Ku Klux Klan 60
Kwong, Lisa 58

Late Rebellion, The (Powell) 73
Lawrence v. Texas 66
Ledford, Katherine 6
LGBTQ+ literature 61–67; Appalachian queerness 53, 61–65; right to same-sex intimacy 66; rights 5, 53, 63–64, 66–67
"Life in the Iron Mills" (Davis) 6–7
Line that Held Us, The (Joy) 12, 41
Linneman, Travis 26
Lioness (Powell) 47–49
"Listening, The" (Roberson) 42
Locklear, Erica Abrams 56
"Lone Grave on the Mountain, The" (Smith) 21
Look Homeward, Angel (Wolfe) 9
Love Child's Hotbed of Occasional Poetry (Finney) 24, 45
Lovesick Blossoms (Watts) 66–67
Lucas, Megan 29

Ma, Lala 39
Madness Like Morning Glories (Davenport) 57
Maimon, Alan 4
Manilla, Marie 22
Marcellus Shale 38
Maren, Mesha 38–40, 62, 64
Masked Man, Black: Pandemic and Protest Poems (Walker) 45, 72
Mathews, Daniel 43
McCarthy, Cormac 1, 11–12
McClanahan, Bill 2, 35
McCollum, Victoria 5, 53
McCrumb, Sharyn 20

McKinney, George 17
McKinney, Gordon B. 20
McLennon, Leigh M. 17
McNally, David 7–8
McNeil, Z. Zane 61
McNeill, Louise 8
Medley, Corina 26
Mehta, Rahul 62–63
Meit, Michael 26
mental health 24–25, 63, 67
Middle Passage 57–58
migration 8–9
military: foreign policy 18, 22, 24; recruitment 17, 22–23; service 18, 22, 24–25, 29; sexual violence 25
Miller, Elizabeth Carolyn 35
mining: *see* fossil fuels
modernity 6, 8–10, 28
Molesky, Jason 38
Monnet, Agnieszka Soltysik 2, 5, 17–18, 28
monsters 1, 3, 5, 7, 10, 21, 25–26, 28, 30–31, 35, 39, 43–44, 58, 60, 67, 71; Monstrocene 71; monstrous 1, 3, 5, 7, 9, 23, 29, 30, 36, 38, 42–43, 49, 62–63, 66–67, 71–73
Mooney, Steve 10
mountains 2, 3, 6–7, 12, 20–21, 30, 36–37, 39, 44, 56; mountain lions 48; mountain people 17, 37, 45
mountaintop removal (MTR) 35–38, 42, 72
"Mountaintops, Appalachia" (Deer Cloud) 36
Musgrove, Brian 28

"Natural Resources" (Null) 46–47
necropolitics 28, 39
neoliberalism 28, 39
Newton, John 58
nightmares 5, 39, 47
No Other World (Mehta) 62–63
Noe, Kenneth W. 17–18
Norman, Gurney 36
Null, Matthew Neill 46–47

Obergefell v. Hodges 66
O'Dell, Tawni 36
Offutt, Chris 26–27, 40–41
oil 8; oil boom 38, boom and bust cycles 7, 38
Otjen, Nathaniel 49
Outer Dark (McCarthy) 1, 11

Page, Myra 8
Palmer, Paulina 62, 67
Pancake, Ann 20–21, 36–38, 49, 59
Pancake, Breece D'J 36
Panowich, Brian 27
Parker, Elizabeth 27
Perdue, Theda 54
Perpetual West (Maren) 64
Phillips, Jayne Anne 22
politics 5, 41, 44–45; far-right populism 43–44, 53
pollution 25, 41, 48
post-Trump moment 4–5, 12, 43–45, 47, 53, 72–73
Potted Meat (Dunn) 22
poverty 17, 19, 26, 29, 58, 61; unemployment 17, 25
Powell, Mark 23–24, 47–49, 73
Provinces of Night (Gay) 12
Purdue Pharma 30, 47

Queer Appalachia 53, 61–63
queer uncanny 67

race 11, 53–61; Appalasian 58–59 (*see also* Black Appalachians and Indigenous Appalachians); equality 8, prejudice 53, 60, 62; racial diversity 53–54, 56–58, 60; racial violence 10; racism 8, 22, 53, 56, 58–60, 73
Rash, Ron 20, 22, 27–29
Redding, Arthur F. 73
Reilly, M. J. 42
religion 28, 65
Return the Innocent Earth (Dykeman) 10–11
Riding the Trail of Tears (Hausman) 54–56
Roberson, Ed 42, 58
Robinson, Richard Knox 1
Ruin 10, 19, 31, 46

Satterwhite, Emily 7
Saunooke Clapsaddle, Annette 54, 56
Say So, The (Franks) 72
Scanlan, Stephen J. 17
Schenkkan, Robert 1
Scott, Rebecca R. 36
settler colonials 1, 6, 35, 53–56, 58
sexual violence 25, 57
shadows 5–6, 8, 12, 20, 26, 37, 41, 45, 56, 58, 63, 66
shale gas development (SGD) 38–40
Sharyn, McCrumb 20
Shelley, Mary 26, 67

INDEX

"Shelton Laurel: 2006" (Rash) 20
Shelton Laurel massacre 20
Shifty's Boys (Offutt) 26, 40–41
Sickels, Carter 62
Sipple, Savannah 65
Skidmore, Hubert 8
Smith, Andrew 43
Smith, Barbara 59
Smith, Effie Waller 21
Somerville, Siobhan 61
South 3–4, 8–10, 17–19, 54, 65, 73; southern gothic 9, 11, 53; southern mountaineer motif 7; southern mountains 2
Southernmost (House) 65
Specter Mountain (Graves and Wright) 25
"Statues of Liberty" (Walker) 58
stereotypes 1, 5, 7, 11, 17, 28, 35, 38, 58–59, 73; hillbilly 1; southern mountaineer 7
Still, James 62
Strange As This Weather Has Been (Pancake) 37–38, 49
Straw, Richard 3
Sugar Run (Maren) 38–39, 64

Tailhook Scandal 25
Tanenbaum, Erin 26
Taylor, Melanie Benson 54
terror 5, 11, 35, 48, 55, 64, 66, 71; terrorized 64
Thomas, Clarence 66–67
Thorpe, Charles 28, 41
Those We Thought We Knew (Joy) 59
"Those Who Are Dead Are Only Now Forgiven" (Rash) 27
Trail of Tears 54–56
Trail of the Lonesome Pine, The (Fox) 7
transatlantic slave trade 58
travel writing 6–12
Trump, Donald 4–5, 26, 43–45, 53, 60, 64, 67, 72; Trump-era horror 5; *see also* politics

Trump country 4, 45, 53; Trumpalachia 4
Truscello, Michael 39
Turner, Daniel Cross 20
Turner, Willian H. 10, 54

uncanny 24, 30, 39, 41, 46, 58, 67
Unquiet Earth, The (Giardina) 36–37
Unrue, Darlene 9
U.S. military service 24
U.S. political system 45
U.S. queer culture 61
U.S. Supreme Court 5, 65–66, 72; *see also* Thomas, Clarence

vampires 19; vampiric 7, 17, 29–30, 35
Vance, J. D. 1, 25, 30–31
Vietnam War 24

Walker, Frank X 11, 29, 45, 57–58, 72
War: Afghanistan War 22; Civil War 17–22, 25; collateral damage 22, 24, 30; geopolitics 23–24; Iraq War 18, 22–25; trauma 17; Vietnam War 24
"Washed Away" (Croley) 37
Water & Power (Dunn) 22, 25
Watts, Julia 66–67
Westengard, Laura 61
Wester, Maisha L. 11, 57–58
What You Are Getting Wrong About Appalachia (Catte) 43
When These Mountains Burn (Joy) 26, 42
Wilber, Tom 38
wildfires 41–45, 49
Wolfe, Thomas 9
World Made Straight, The (Rash) 20
Wuerthner, George 30
WWJD (Sipple) 65

zombies 17, 19, 27–28; blind zombification 28; living dead 36; undead 18–19

Milton Keynes UK
Ingram Content Group UK Ltd.
UKHW031841280724
446193UK00001B/49